WIGFIELD

WIGFIELD

THE CAN-DO TOWN THAT JUST MAY NOT

AMY SEDARIS   PAUL DINELLO   STEPHEN COLBERT

PHOTOGRAPHS BY TODD OLDHAM

HYPERION   NEW YORK

Library of Congress Cataloging-in-Publication Data

Sedaris, Amy.
    Wigfield / Amy Sedaris, Paul Dinello, and Stephen Colbert ; photographs by Todd Oldham.—1st ed.
        p. cm.
    ISBN 0-7868-6812-0
    1. City and town life—Fiction. 2. Journalists—Fiction. I. Dinello, Paul. II. Colbert, Stephen, 1964- III. Title.

PS3619.E34 W5 2003
813'.6—dc21

2002192212

Hyperion books are available for special promotions and premiums. For details contact Hyperion Special Markets, 77 West 66th Street, 11th floor, New York, New York 10023, or call 212-456-0133.

FIRST EDITION

10 9 8 7 6 5 4 3 2 1

"Words cannot describe all the things that I have left to write."

—Russell Hokes

DEDICATION

As this book, including this dedication, was written
in chronological order, I have, so far, only myself to thank.
This is assuming I will continue to be involved.

PREFACE

(See Introduction.)

INTRODUCTION

RIOR to embarking on the voyage of discovery that is this book, a quick but gripping note about me:

My name is Russell Hokes, author. But long before I became a writer, I wasn't one. I worked for the Federal Department of Transportation painting the center lines on interstates. It was rewarding work, with the added benefit of being unchallenging. But following a heated dispute with my foreman over the meaning of the word *sick day*, I quit my job shortly after he fired me. For the first time in my life I was truly free. But freedom has its price, which I soon found out was money. So, much like a butcher naturally becomes a surgeon, or a boxer becomes a cop, I decided to apply my knowledge of drawing long white lines on asphalt to drawing much shorter ones with loops and curls on paper. In short, words. I became a writer!

A writer. The vision of my new life hung before me: Encamped, nay, ensconced in my cozy mountain cabin-mansion, the fire roaring, the wind howling, the words flowing, I would make a name for myself like Hemingway. My only concern would be finding time to write with all the skiing, hunting, and hobnobbing with the New York literotica I'd be doing. I'd be rubbing elbows and other sensitive parts with the cultural elite, quipping charmingly to the encircling bevy of literary ingenues. Late nights spent sipping from tankards of sloe gin fizzes, raging and railing about the hypocrisies of our times, then on to the next book signing. Another town, another series of women. How long can I keep up this pace? I must get back to my art, my writing!

But how can I? I'm sucked dry by the parasites who cling to my every preposition. Suddenly it's not fun anymore. I've been blocked for days, weeks, months! I stare at my stack of books, my past works, conquests that now mock me like ungrateful children. Shut up! Shut your mouths! I created you! I grab my head in torment. I gulp down the bourbon desperately trying to anesthetize the demons. The liquor flows down my gullet like the river Styx but does not bestow the forgetful darkness. It merely amplifies the voices, the voices, the voices! Is there no rest? No escape? I stumble to the closet and reach in for my salvation. I see it all so clearly now—I'll follow Papa Hemingway to the happy hunting grounds with a one-way ticket on the Lead Bullet Express over Gun Powder Falls through Massive Head Wound Canyon. I raise the barrel with trembling hands to my quivering mouth, standing on my shaking legs on top of a wobbly table. My resolve stiffens as my trigger finger firms. I set like stone as my blood freezes, and my heart hardens—petrified! The trigger clicks, the hammer falls, the bullet flies, and the brightest light in the literary heavens is quenched forever. . . .

But first I needed an idea and a healthy advance.

As receiving payment for work I had already done had always proved a difficult enough task for me, being paid for work I had not yet done nor had the skill to accomplish should have proven to be an impossible quest. But a journey of a thousand miles starts with a single misstep. I decided my first work of fiction would be my résumé.

RUSSELL HOKES

39 SALINGER STREET
FAMOUS WRITERS COLONY
FAULKNER, MAINE
HOME PHONE: OUT OF ORDER, SORRY

OBJECTIVE

To write a book, other than the ones that I have already written, so that I may use my words like a sword of swift justice in service of the truth, but in an easy-to-read, highly marketable way.

QUALIFICATIONS

I am a strong candidate for the position that I am applying for because my words explode off the page like electric action to maximize the impact. That is how I describe my background and strengths. This section is concise and contains action words, and should sell my most marketable experiences and abilities.

EDUCATION

- *Miss Brontë's Toddler Time*,
  NURSERY THRU PRE-K—
  mastered use of blocks, played well with some

- *Ralph Waldo Emerson Lake and Palmer Elementary*,
  K THRU 8TH GRADE—
  achieved full course of immunizations

- *Harry Potter High School*,
  9TH THRU 14TH GRADES—
  fiction club, nonfiction club, how-to and miscellaneous club, cookbooks club, poetry club, voted most likely to publish a best-seller, graduated valedictorian and salutatorian, with *honors*

▸ *Heidelberg University,*
UNDER- AND SUBGRADUATE WORK—
AREAS OF FOCI:
writing, English, English writers, and writing English;
graduated magna cum laude and summa cum laude; also
received dueling scar

▸ *Oxford-upon-Cambridge,*
POST- AND APRÈS-GRADUATE STUDIES—
doctoral thesis under tutelage of Scott Turow, Stephen
King, Jackie Collins, and the guy who wrote those
"Chicken Soup" self-help books

EXPERIENCE

▸ ASSISTANT VISITING ADJUNCT ASSOCIATE
PROFESSOR EMERITUS OF BEST-SELLING BOOKS,
University of Bogotá (defunct)
In the same manner as above, I would like to describe my
job responsibilities. I will be concise and remove all
unnecessary words and/or phrases, including the specific
results of my actions or decisions to demonstrate my
contribution. Thank you.

Best-Selling Author. Employer: The Public
▸ *The Guinness Book of World Records*
▸ *Fortune Cookies* (Szechwan-U.S.)
▸ *Fortune Cookies* (Hunan-Canada/Alaska)

Honors.
▸ Pulitzer Prize for fiction—first runner up
▸ Nobel Prize in literature—missed plane to
Stockholm—could have won, don't know
▸ National Book Award—presenter (wore my
own tux)

REFERENCES

*Encyclopaedia Britannica, Roget's Thesaurus, World Almanac
1992*

SPECIAL SKILLS

*Typing, making deadlines, being reasonable about rewrites,
ability to churn out best-sellers, and juggling*

(Note to Publisher: I include this confessional information about my qualifications for two reasons. [1] Now that I am a legitimate writer, I'm sure we can all laugh at what was at the time a gross misrepresentation of my abilities. Ha-ha. [2] I would like you to judge this book in the context of my actual experience and not on what I told you was my experience. To recap: I have no experience.)

My résumé was the foot in the door that the rest of my body so desperately needed. I secured a meeting with Hyperion Books. After regaling the assembled editors with details about the world's longest fingernails came the hard part: selling an idea that I neither had nor was likely to acquire. But like a blind, machete-wielding explorer on the fringe of the Amazon, I simply plunged in.

"Book," I said. "I want to write a book."

"About what?" they cunningly retorted.

Checkmate. As I started to eye the exits I said, "Knights of the Round Table! Does that excite you?"

"Nope."

"Then that's not it." I sidled toward the door.

"Well, what is it about?"

"Guess." I favored them with an impish grin as I felt for the door handle.

"Is it about small-town life?"

Daylight? "Why do you ask?"

"Well, we've been considering a series on the disappearing American main street."

Tiptoeing back to the table. "You're getting warmer . . . keep going."

"Is it a book about the shattered illusions, and . . . uh . . ."

"Warmer . . ."

". . . brave lives of small-town residents?"

Pounding my fist. "C'mon people! Jump in here, help him out!"

". . . that celebrates what is best in America?"

"Yes! You're on fire!"

". . . by showing the indomitable human spirit in times of crisis?"

"Bingo! Jackpot! Ding! Ding! Ding! You people get me!"

With a sizable advance clenched in my tiny fist, I sallied forth to write a book about the small-town experience. I quickly realized that this idea for a book—"my idea" as it quickly came to be known in my elite inner circle—fit me like a glove, with the idea being the hand. Well, actually, I suppose I should be the hand, or rather my hand should be the hand. The idea should be the glove. The point is, my idea was an idea that I actually knew something about.

Here was something I could write. I had already experienced many small towns. During my numerous years at the Department of Transportation I had the chance to spend a large amount of time spending a lot of time in a large amount of our small towns, and often each town's different story was the same. These towns scrambled to exist, like a small, helpless animal trapped beneath my foot. It just wouldn't stay out of my geraniums. I've seen communities fold like a gut-shot Oswald. And, each time, who was the Jack Ruby? The government. I've witnessed towns die when regulators closed the local arsenic factory, or health officials chained the gates on the mercury dispersal plant. I've seen the hollow, empty eyes of desperate people staggering under the weight of debt and twisting with the agony of poverty. And now I could make money off of having seen that. Finally, a job I was qualified for!

My book would be written from the heart, probably my own. I would talk about how the death of Small-Town America brings great pain to me because

I had always had an appreciation for these tiny villages. For who doesn't feel a fondness for a place where you know all your neighbors, and you can keep your doors unlocked, or you could enter your neighbors' home at night because you know his doors are unlocked? I would tell their story. After a lengthy vacation in the Yucatán, that is exactly what I planned to do. Deadlines be damned—I needed some *me* time!

Returning from an ill-fated jaunt in Cabo San Cabo (which included a short but brutal stay at the Hacienda del Policia), I was a wiser yet poorer man. With that behind me, I took what was left of my advance and began my research for Life in Small-Town America. I decided to hit the library first and was shocked to find the large amount of resource information available and how well-trod this subject was. What I learned made me angry. What I read made me sleepy. Here is what I remember:

Small towns are America's most precious commodity behind pork bellies and clean burning coal. Statistics show that shortly after World War Two, America consisted of A Lot of small towns. Today that number stands at A Little. Tomorrow, who knows? Less than A Little? Perhaps A Few?

One can only imagine how many more statistics could be gleaned from those library books piled in my garage. We know statistics don't lie: Chickens lay eggs. A man is hanged, not hung. Both deer and shrimp are plural. But it came time to find a more experiential experience, one that involved less reading. A statistic I could touch, or feel, or hold. It didn't matter what it was as long as I didn't have to read it. The point is: I hate reading. With the county library hot on my trail, I pulled up stakes and set down roots in my car.

With my future in my rearview mirror, I set a course for the past. I was searching for a simpler time, a simpler people. I threw out my anchor and set sail for Small-Town America. Where would I go? How would I stop? When would I eat?

For the first three hundred or so miles, I admired my work: The Painted Center Line. Often the solid white, occasionally the double yellow, but most often the broken white. Space, line, space, line. It penetrates the mind. Dot, dash, dot, dash, dot, dash. Like Morse code, America's vast interstate highway system was tapping out a message to me and me alone. Literally translated from the Morse it would be, "A . . . A . . . A . . . A . . . A . . . A . . . A . . . A," as if America had something it desperately wanted to say but was hampered by a pronounced stutter. Still, I heard her loud and clear. America was asking, "Why did you contribute to a road system that was built to circumvent our Small Towns?"

Begun in 1952, the interstate system was, according to *Roget's Thesaurus*, touted as a panacea for a rubric of our omnibus of catchalls. In truth it was a system spearheaded by the Military Industrial Complex, so that Uncle Sam could move large numbers of troops, tanks, and nuclear weapons. It also added an economic boon to our interstate commerce system, as well as providing an inexpensive and safe means of travel for our increasingly prosperous society. In short, there was no downside, but at what cost? No longer was the traveler routed through what its critics called "anemic little tourist traps" like Stump Hole, or Bucklick. These towns and many others became spectral apparitions of their former ghostly selves. (*Ibid.*: *Roget's*.) (Re: Ibid.—See *The Elements of Style*.)

I had been on the road for what seemed like weeks but was probably closer to days, more specifically hours. I needed an angle for my book, but all I had was anger. I traveled from one small town to another, so many that they began to blend into one big town. For each place I visited, I followed a strict research protocol. I'd usually pull in during breakfast time where I would patronize a charming local diner with mom-and-pop names like Denny's or Shoneys or Denny's. Once there, my ritual was the same: three eggs over easy, hash browns, wheat toast (buttered), links if they got 'em, coffee black with a side of cream. Then it was over to the motel for a nap. Rising fresh at the crack of lunch, I wandered the town in search of a story. Always my search would lead me to a lunch counter where I could utilize my power of observation as I observed myself consuming a Reuben, a plate of fries, a roll (with butter), a soda (almost exclusively of the cola variety), and for dessert, a buttered piece of pie. As I laid my head in my folded arms, I would try to unlock the mystery of the town. What was its secret? Why am I so sleepy? My God, I can barely keep my eyes open. So, it was back to the motel for a little informative television. So many stories, so well told. A large portion of what little was left of my advance went to my Pay-Per-View research, but they would always cut away before the money shot.

Then it was back out into the breach for dinner. A steak, potato usually baked, liberally buttered, and bourbon—the idea fuel. I'd look around at the other diners thinking there must be a book's worth of material just in this room, if only someone would write it and put my name on it. To end the evening, I'd spend time in a neighborhood drinkery, soaking up the local culture with my eyes and alcohol with my liver. A bar maid would turn down my request for a personal in-depth interview with a gentle protest, or more often a slap, then it was back to the motel for a little snack and a lot of sleep. Each afternoon, while the complimentary security guard wake-up call was pounding on my door, I would quickly gather my belongings, check out through the bathroom window, and then shamble to the car.

With the remainder of my advance jingling in my pocket and a looming deadline, I desperately needed to make some headway. How I pined for the days of the open road, just me and my paintbrush and our beautiful white center lines. I was in a quandary. What should be my next move? Where should be my next stop? Having no answers, I couldn't make up my mind, but my alternator turned out to be very decisive.

Broken down on the side of the interstate somewhere between Hell and a Hard Place, I spied a charming little hamlet peeking through a pile of used tires. Was this to be my Shangri-la, or my Waterloo? I was determined to find out. So, being fleet of foot and swift of deft, I climbed over a guardrail, scrambled down a gravel embankment, and crawled under a rusting chain-link fence emblazoned with a faded sign proudly proclaiming DO NOT ENTER BY ORDER OF THE CORPS OF ENGINEERS, and took my first steps into town. Would I find the fading jewel of Americana? Would I find my small-town Atlantis quivering on the brink of annihilation by an indifferent federal government? And perhaps most important, would I find a rebuilt alternator and someone who would take a personal check?

But what and where was I? And who were these people? And how? The answer to the riddle was contained in a clue to its solution. WIGFIELD, said the sign. WIGFIELD'S HOTTEST LADIES.

I was intrigued. When was it incorporated? What was its population? And just how hot were these ladies? The first two questions seemed to lose importance after I raised the third. So, to fight my natural inclination not to finish anything I've ever started, I decided to answer the last question first. Unfortunately, the solution required a cover charge, and the mystery remained. I did, however, learn that bouncers are a humorless, violent sort. That left the first two questions. But what were they? I haven't been paying attention.

I decided to investigate the town and gather information.

Wigfield is a quarter-mile stretch of highway known as Wigfield. It's the kind of place that if a person were in a car not paying attention he'd probably pass through never realizing what he missed. Or if a person were driving through and paying attention he might drive faster hoping to ignore what he had just seen. Like the peanut concealed under the street hustler's walnut shell, so is Wigfield difficult to find and likely to cost you forty bucks. As is the case with many small towns, Wigfield is totally isolated, with the exception of the four-lane interstate that runs parallel to its Main (and only) Street.

I walked down the road staring into the shops searching for something in this town to tell me its story. I read the signs hanging in storefront windows hoping a tale of drama would emerge: DAM BEING TORN DOWN SALE! declared the first. EVERYTHING MUST GO BEFORE THE DAM IS TORN DOWN AND TOWN IS DESTROYED, trumpeted another. PREFLOOD SALE, screamed a third. Then, like a golfer playing the back nine trying to finish before the heavy stuff comes down, I was struck with a lightning bolt. My God! That's it! That's my story . . .

SMALL TOWNS ARE A BARGAIN HUNTER'S DREAM!

I scrambled down to the end of the main street. I pulled out my notepad and like a retiree standing before the chrome spout of a spinning slot machine with her hands cupped, I stood poised to catch the flood of ideas that would surely come pouring out. My thoughts quickly turned to prayer. "Oh Lord, please give my hand the added strength and agility to move my pencil swiftly enough to keep pace with my surging vision. Amen." Nothing. "Lord? Perhaps I put the cart before the vision. Let me quickly rephrase my prayer. First, please give me the surging vision that my hand can't keep up with, and then the ability to keep up with it. Sorry for the confusion. Okay, let it rip. Amen." Still Nothing. The Lord, like every woman I have ever known, was cold and distant.

I started to rethink my breakthrough. Perhaps the fact that this town was a shopper's paradise was not my holy grail. But what then? Time, like a sizable advance a publisher might give you, was quickly slipping through my fingers. I then looked up into the sky and beheld a giant looming behemoth. I dropped to the extremely warm dirt in awe, gazing up at this enormous concrete wonder as if it were one of America's famous landmarks. But unlike those unforgettable American monuments—the metal statue of the lady, that big hole in the ground, and the mountain with the faces on it—the name of this one remained shrouded in mystery. Where did it come from, and more important, how did it get here? Was it a natural formation? Or, as seemed more likely, was it erected by ancient alien astronauts who were getting kickbacks from a concrete distributor?

Maybe the huge metal letters riveted to its surface would shed some light on the mystery: ALFONSE T. BULKWALLER MEMORIAL DAM. Jackpot! A giant concrete dam built on top of a tiny river. The pieces were falling into place. I felt hypnotized sitting in its shadow. Somehow, a dam seemed fitting. It represented what I imagined was happening inside my skull, as if there were a concrete barricade erected along my river of ideas, not allowing them to flow. I focused on the dam again. I noticed it was decorated with spray-painted lettering. Perhaps these were pleas scrawled by the townspeople. The words spoke to me as if I were reading them:

"DON'T FLOOD OUR TOWN!"
"STOP BILL FARBER FROM TEARING DOWN THIS DAM!"
"I DID REGINA AT THE TOP IN THE BOTTOM."

Wait a minute . . . Thoughts were trying to form. The wheels in my skull were turning like millstones, and my brain was the grist. Large dam . . . small town in front of dam . . . water behind dam . . . take down dam equals . . .

think . . . what? . . . remember signs in shops . . . preflood sale . . . don't flood our town . . . I was so close! Like mold on cheese, a complete idea began to grow. Mold . . . cheese . . . melty . . . cheddar cheese fries . . . delicious . . .

No! Must stay focused . . . dam . . . torn down . . . rushing water . . . town . . . flood . . . *Yes*!

A SMALL TOWN IN PERIL, THREATENED BY A DAM THE GOVERNMENT IS GOING TO TEAR DOWN!

So perfect, as if I were making it up, which I was moments away from doing. Wigfield is endangered! But how? I knew that in order to fully understand Wigfield's present plight, I would have to delve into its past. This decision was partly based on my journalistic instinct, but mostly on the fact that nestled inside a plastic bucket riveted to the side of the dam was a stack of historical pamphlets put out by the Bureau for the Reclamation of Natural Landmarks, the government agency that oversaw the building of the dam. It is this trifold document that I paraphrase here in its entirety.

BUREAU FOR THE RECLAMATION OF NATURAL LANDMARKS

Information About the Bulkwaller Dam

Welcome to the Alfonse T. Bulkwaller Memorial Dam. In 1931, during the height of the low point of the Depression, Senator Alfonse T. Bulkwaller declared his intentions to raise the dam as a testimony to our country's ability to construct monolithic concrete structures in the midst of adverse conditions. The dam was to be, according to its designer, Teddy Bulkwaller,

"A structure so magnificent that it rivals any creation that God has put on this earth, thereby causing angels to weep with the knowledge that our Savior has been bested!" Upon passage of the funding appropriations bill, thousands of unemployable, unskilled relatives of Alfonse Bulkwaller came to the Fresh Springs Water Basin to build what would become the World's Densest Dam.

FUN FACT:

There is enough concrete in the Bulkwaller Dam (4.8 million cubic yards) to build a vertical highway as wide as the dam that would reach all the way to the top!

Before construction could begin, however, workers had to divert the Fresh Springs Creek back onto itself. To accomplish this feat, workers began random blasting of the entire area using dynamite. For the next eight months, workers ignited sixty tons of explosives, leveling the area and displacing enough dirt and rock to feed Sub-Saharan Africa. Eventually, a few light boulders were placed upstream in the creek's path, which successfully stopped the flow. Workers spent another three months blasting the area, and then building started. The engineers' vision was a simple one: construct a concrete bulwark between the sheer cliffs of the majestic Fresh Springs Gorge. The greatest challenge would be the construction of the cliffs and the gorge.

FUN FACT:

More men died in the building of the Bulkwaller Dam than at the Battle of Shiloh.

In the interest of safety, Bulkwaller insisted on using three times more concrete than engineers thought was called for. Luckily, the supply of this endless stream of cement was never in question, thanks to the close ties Senator Bulkwaller had established with his own concrete company.

FUN FACT:

The Bulkwaller Dam is so thick and heavy, if it were to fall onto itself it would crush both its original self as well as its falling counterpart.

The first structures to be built were the temporary housing units where the thousands of workers would live during the decades of construction. The laborers were invited to submit housing ideas. These included: neoclassical structures with ionic pillars framing large screened-in porches, colonial-style homes, and Prairie-style houses with large fireplaces and stained-glass windows. Eventually it was decided, with input from the senator himself, that each residence would consist of two pieces of plywood nailed together in an A-frame and covered with corrugated tin.

FUN FACT:

Upon completion of the dam, hard hats emblazoned with the words Bulkwaller Dam *were handed out as rewards to any construction workers who hadn't died of head injuries.*

Before a single foot of the dam could be laid, unprecedented volumes of concrete needed to be mixed. Concrete consists of eight ingredients—water, crushed rock, loose rock, tiny rocks, pebbles, crushed pebbles, flattened boulders, and crushed loose flattened boulders. These must be mixed in the proper proportions to yield strong concrete. Rock is probably the most important part of cement, making up, after the water evaporates, 100 percent of the material. A nearby source of rock needed to be found. Eventually, prospecting parties discovered that the proposed dam site was sitting on a sheet of bedrock. Blasting began again.

After months of exploding the ground, it was believed that enough rock had been collected to mix the necessary cement to build the dam. Now, the workforce was split into two groups. One had the job of hauling the many tons of crumbled stone to the screening plants, the other, hauling the many exploded workers to a makeshift morgue.

FUN FACT:

Bulkwaller Dam's structural volume surpasses the largest pyramid in Egypt, and its burial chambers are filled with treasures beyond the pharaohs' wildest dreams.

At the screening plant, three screening towers separated the rock into different sizes; fine, minute, and petite. Anything over two inches in diameter was strapped with dynamite and exploded. The crushed rock was then carted by rail to the site in large concrete tubs. To transport the stone to make the cement for the tubs, concrete chutes were used. Flatcars made from concrete conveyed the rock that was mixed to make the chutes. Concrete buckets running on zip lines moved the crushed aggregate needed to make the flatcars. How the rock was moved to create the concrete buckets is a mystery to this day.

FUN FACT:

If all the copper wiring used in the Bulkwaller Dam were laid end to end it would reach less than an inch. There is no copper wire in the Bulkwaller Dam.

The concrete needed to be mixed at water level. Unfortunately, the only water in the area was the Fresh Springs Creek, which had been dammed with boulders, allowing no water to flow to the site. Blasting began again. With the boulders pulverized, the river began to flow. A large supply of concrete was mixed, but before it could be poured, the river needed to be diverted again, and the area dried by a brigade of immigrant squeegee men using rags and sponges to sop up the moisture. While the area was prepared, the wet concrete was stored at the mixing plant. Unfortunately, in the time it took to dry the riverbed, the concrete had set, so the process was repeated, until it became apparent that there was no way to mix the cement and then dry the area before the concrete set. During these many attempts the mixing *plant became filled, wall to wall, floor to ceiling, with hardened cement tubs of concrete. It was discovered, however, that, thanks to a brilliant stroke of incompetence, the factory was built without a foundation, thereby allowing engineers to slide a set of sled skids underneath the building and then haul the entire structure into the river, where it was bolted to the bedrock. Dam complete.*

FUN FACT:

If the Bulkwaller Dam was mechanically animated and fitted with a giant robot brain, it would successfully conquer the planet, forcing enslaved humans to work in its vast network of zinc mines. It could not be stopped!

This pamphlet is reprinted courtesy of the Bureau for the Reclamation of Natural Landmarks.

And so it was the creation of this mighty stone colossus that created the dry riverbed up from which sprang, like a mushroom from manure, the small town of Wigfield.

Cartographically, Wigfield is an enigma appearing on no official document. On most highway maps, the area is whimsically listed only as "Proposed Super Fund Site 554," a mark of shame the residents here wear with pride. The prevailing architecture is best described as "hasty." Many's the load-bearing wall here that could easily be patched with corrugated cardboard and a staple gun. In exterior construction, the designers clearly were not skittish about using native materials, such as traffic cones and sawhorses, thus creating a charming architectural mélange, the overall effect being that of a series of children's forts made from stolen highway equipment.

Geographically, Wigfield can be imagined as a narrow dusty plain, a barren man-made ditch situated between two gravel-covered banks, the edges of which are thick with brush like the beard on a pirate on shore leave who won't take no for an answer. In the distance, toward the south entrance to town, loom two great mountains, their lofty peaks jousting with the clouds. Upon closer inspection, however, these are revealed to be three-story slag piles, smoking with chemical fires that local folklore says can never be extinguished unless God himself should shed tears upon them.

But what of the people? To casual observers they might appear gaunt and leathery, but a more informed glance confirms this. In bearing, they are suspiciously judgmental, in expression warily guarded, in speech colorfully vulgar.

But things are not as rosy as they seem.

The government has decided to tear down the Alfonse T. Bulkwaller Memorial Dam, flooding this dwarfish pueblo. Leading the charge is State Representative Bill Farber, who argues that the dam was built as a make-work project, provides no irrigation and generates no power, and that the dam's builders never took into account the ecological damage it was doing. While it might be true that in tearing down the dam the gains are obvious—restoring the salmon run, raising the water table (which is dangerously low), and providing fresh water for thousands of people downstream—what is lost is not so obvious. Most people probably couldn't put their finger on it. Even a carefully selected panel of highly trained experts using the latest finger-putting-on technology probably couldn't.

Hopefully this book will. At least that's what I've promised my publisher.

Because this book has to be far more than just words on paper between two stylishly art-directed covers. It has to be at least 50,000 of them contractually, or I don't get paid. So far . . . let's see . . . 5,314. My God. Is that all?&! My fingers are bloody, my eyes half-mast. So instead of me rattling on, I've decided to let the town residents tell their story in their own words. Because, frankly, I'm out.

CHAPTER ONE

❧

Iꜰ this book was ever to be more than a contractually obligated pipe dream, I knew I had to gain the townspeople's trust, a trust I had not earned and had no plans to. But where to start? How to make first contact?

It's a curious thing to try to reach out to strangers. Nature, by its very nature, makes this seem unnatural. Take the animal kingdom as an example. The act of reaching out to another person has inherent in it an aggression, a threat of violence. As we know, each human has his or her personal space. (Mine happens to be very close to my body, but very tall—almost eighty-five feet. For instance, I find it very difficult to stand underneath a tree if it's full of people.) To compensate for their skittishness around one another, humans have developed an elaborate system of body language. Folded arms, for instance, may signal that the subject is closed off and wishes for the conversation to end, or that he is an Indian chief. Either way, avoid these people. A woman with her legs splayed wide may be saying "Welcome. How do you do?" or "I am adventurous and open to new ideas." Either way, seek these women out.

But most difficult of all is the approach of a stranger. The unsolicited sideways shuffle of the unknown. Is that a knife in his hand or an ice cream cone? You never know until you taste it. The ratlike fear grips your hind brain and drives you up against the wall searching desperately for any exit, any weapon. You lash out with the strength of a madman, slashing with bits of broken glass, howling in your fright turned rage, the fight-or-flight reflex turning you into an unstoppable blood-lusting wolverine, until panting, you stand triumphantly looking down at the mangled remains of the stranger. OK. It was a just an ice cream cone . . . this time.

And was I not a stranger in this strange land? There was nothing about my manner or dress I would trust. Why should they? I could be just another journalist swooping down on a small town to feed on the residents' grief, exploiting the misfortune of the unfortunate for my own personal financial gain. God, I hope they trust me.

I decided that an open, forthright approach would be the most disarming. A smile on my face, eyes wide open and receptive. My arms and legs akimbo. I wandered the streets thusly for more than a minute until I blew out a kneecap and the unprecedented dryness of my eyeballs forced me to blink. I decided to go with Plan B. There is a hard-and-fast rule in the journalism biz: Always have a Plan B. This rule never seemed more important than at the moment I, limping badly and rubbing my eyes, realized I had no Plan B.

In some societies it is appropriate for men to weep publicly. The derisive taunting of the passersby made it abundantly clear that this was not one of them. Nevertheless, I sank to the curbside and held my head in my hands and just let go of all the pressure that had been eating me alive for the last several minutes. Then I heard a voice that fell like rain down the gutter of my ears, a voice that soothed like a mother's to her child lost at the mall.

"I'm gonna have to ask you to get off our property."

I looked up to see an elderly couple in their late thirties. Evidently I was lounging in their carport. I quickly explained what had brought me to this place, and when I mentioned the book I was writing they lit up like Buddhist monks. They were eager to talk about the town they loved. They welcomed me into their little ranch house, where I welcomed myself into their refrigerator. While they both talked and took notes, I ate lunch and cocked an ear.

UDELL & ELEANOR GRIMMETT

Udell: "I'm Udell, and this is Eleanor. We're the Grimmetts. We've been married for eighteen years. We met right here in Wigfield!"

Eleanor: "I used to work at the counter at the drugstore."

Udell: "And I was mighty fond of pie!"

Eleanor: "He sure was! Every day he'd come into the drugstore and sit in the same seat at the counter."

Udell: "I love a good counter."

Eleanor: "He'd look so handsome in his uniform."

Udell: "Eleanor! It wasn't really a uniform, it was more of a protective jumpsuit."

Eleanor: "Well, whatever it was, you looked handsome!"

Udell: "I suppose. I'm the luckiest fella in town!"

Eleanor: "Getting back to the pie. He'd come in and have his pie, and he would tell me jokes. He was so funny and handsome. Tell him one!"

Udell: "All right. I will. What did the door say to the wall? Give up? 'Can you help me out here? I'm in a bit of a jam.' "

(Author's note: I don't get it.)

Eleanor: "He should be on TV. Anyway, one day he came in like he always does, and he called me over and said he couldn't eat the pie because something was in it."

Udell: (laughs) "She fell for it!"

Eleanor: "I got worried, because this wouldn't be the first time we had found something unpleasant in one of our pies. So I started picking through the dessert with his fork and lo and behold I found this ring! We never even went on a date!"

Udell: "Not a one!" ·

Eleanor: "We were married by the justice the next week . . ."

Udell: "And we've been married ever since, and here's the secret: A wife has to be respected like a living thing. The day I got married I learned that, and that's why we've been married so long." ·

Eleanor: "I never even kissed another man."

Udell: "Damn right. That makes two of us."

Eleanor: "And we settled down here in Wigfield."

Udell: "We tried living other places."

Eleanor: "Udell's job kept moving . . ."

Udell: "Every time the plutonium storage ditch would get full, we'd have to relocate."

Eleanor: "We lived at the north end of town . . ."

Udell: "Wigfield Heights . . ."

Eleanor: "Over by the abutment . . ."

Udell: "Wiglette Park . . ."

Eleanor: "Where were we living when you almost choked to death on all those mints?"

Udell: "Eleanor . . ."

Eleanor: "He thought they were aspirins, and he's prone to headaches. Can't keep a pill in the house. Udell just pops them like peanuts."

Udell: "Point is, we're happy here. I couldn't imagine living anywhere else but Wigfield. I guess we're just small-town folks. That's why this town means so much to us. It's sad to see things change."

Eleanor: "Life was so much easier. Udell used to come home from work, and after we'd burned his clothes we'd go for a walk to enjoy the warm evening."

Udell: "Here's a little something you probably didn't know: Even in the dead of winter, the ground here is always a constant 78 degrees. Of course, in the summer months it goes up to about 140."

Eleanor: "God knows we've melted more than one pair of sneakers."

Udell: "Anyway. One day, out of nowhere, some pantywaist government regulator pinheads decided it was in the 'best interest of living creatures' to shut down the plutonium ditch. The only upside about the ditch closing was that it filled with groundwater, and now, when the wind is right, the whole town is covered in a glowing ditch fog. It's like sitting in a sauna. The best part is food stays fresher. We don't even have to wrap it."

Eleanor: "Meat doesn't go bad here, even if you leave it on the counter for days."

Udell: "I guess that's just another advantage of living in a small town."

Eleanor: "After the government closed the ditch, Udell lost his job."

Udell: "Now they want to tear down the dam!"

Eleanor: "He started drinking heavily and treating me poorly. Eventually I took a couple of stabs at suicide."

Udell: "But we both know that suicide isn't the answer. I always tell her, 'Only cowards commits suicide . . . '"

Eleanor: "That's true."

Udell: ". . . and only cowards don't.' "

Eleanor: "Anyway, Udell's drinkin' got pretty ugly. This one time we got into a horrible argument. I told him I was going for a drive. I grabbed the car keys and stormed out of the house, then I stormed back in. We lived in an RV at the time."

Udell: "I guess I did tip a few too many back."

Eleanor: "To the point of blackouts."

Udell: (laughs) "Yeah, I lost a lot of time."

Eleanor: "He'd come home early in the morning, clothes disheveled, speckled with blood."

Udell: "She'd hold up the newspaper and point to a story about another body found in a shallow grave and say, 'Did you do this?' And I would smile back and shrug my shoulders and say, 'I really don't know.' Because I didn't." (laughs)

Eleanor: "They blamed it on the Maniac. Oh, you probably never heard of the Wigfield Maniac—or 'acs,' as the case may be. We keep it kind of hush-hush. We don't want to hurt the tourist trade."

Udell: "There's no need to make a major case out of it. Every small town has its shortcomings. Some small towns have a problem with the kids running off to the big city, other small towns might have worries about a drought affecting the crops, one of ours just happens to be a mindless killing machine who feeds on our fear."

Eleanor: "But enough about us."

Udell: "You spending the night?"

Eleanor: "He could stay in Charlie's old room!"

Udell: "Eleanor! The dogs are in there!"

Eleanor: "You're not being very hospitable."

Udell: "You're right. Please stay, you can have . . . uh . . . that room."

Eleanor: "We could help you with the book! We know everybody in town!"

Udell: "This fella should talk to Fleet."

Eleanor: "Absolutely! Fleet Hollinger practically runs this town, and he's one of our mayors."

Udell: "That's something else you don't know about Wigfield: We have three mayors! How many towns can say that?"

Eleanor: "It was a happy accident!"

Udell: "Yeah, except for all those people that got hurt."

Eleanor: "Fleet owned the plutonium ditch where Udell worked."

Udell: "Well, technically he owned the ditch, the plutonium
belonged to an independent contractor."

Eleanor: "Please say you'll stay."

I quickly accepted. What's a better example of what's precious about
small-town life than me taking the Grimmetts up on their offer for a free
place to stay? That's why small towns must be preserved. I only hoped that I
would continue to see small-town charms exhibited in the form of free food
and possibly some spending cash. It was difficult for me to tell the Grimmetts
how long I would need to stay. Having never written a book before, I had no
way to gauge the time it would take to complete a 50,000-word tome. And
then the realization hit me: I could be at this for days! In a panic, soaking in
my quickly forming flop sweat, I realized that I might never have the energy in
the form of time to interview everyone in the town. I considered sending out
a questionnaire. Here's a sampling of the questions:

1. If you had to write a book about this town and it had to be done
quickly, what would you write? Be specific! Support your answer in
50,000 words or more.

2. If you were sending out a questionnaire to people who lived in a
town that was threatened by the proposed tearing down of its dam, what
would you ask?

But then, like a sign from shouting angels madly waving their arms from heaven, I remembered the words of Flannery O'Connor I read once on the back of an herbal tea box: "Writing is a terrible experience, during which the hair often falls out and the teeth decay." Questionnaires only meant more writing. I must stick to my original plan: Meet these good people face-to-face and corral their words into a book written by me. I told the Grimmetts I would be back around dinnertime or possibly lunch, whichever came first, and set forth to meet the People of Wigfield.

CHAPTER TWO

MY research led me almost immediately to one of the numerous gentlemen's clubs in town. I arrived at Tit Time around eleven A.M. Why Tit Time? I suppose it was the cunning way they incorporated the large female breasts into the establishment's name on the sign. Poetically dotting each *i* was a single robust teat, which together formed the requisite pair. This indicated to me a level of class and sophistication one does not normally associate with the flesh trade. Manning the door was a colorful fella. In lieu of the cover charge, I offered the information that I was writing a book about the town. My wallet untouched, I entered, slightly stunned, through the doors, pondering how many other forms of adult entertainment could come my way for no cost now that I'm writer. Once inside, I immediately took notice of the upbeat disco versions of southern rock. As the anthems invited me into the smoky darkness, my attention was drawn to the focal point of the room: the runway—a ten-foot-long fiberboard platform painted black and tastefully aproned with red-and-green plastic tiki grass. The lip of the stage had been further accented with lengths of chaser light tubing firmly staple-gunned into place. And in an admirable display of economy, the stage was built around the club's main support column, which had been spray-painted gold and now cleverly doubled as the dancer's pole. In response to my presence, a working gal, her loins clad in what from a distance appeared to be fringe, hoisted herself onstage and began to dance, or more accurately shift her weight from foot to foot.

After a lengthy table dance interview, with full release, I sat down at the bar to replenish my fluids. The publican was a dense-browed, heavy-lipped, thick-necked gentleman who served my drink with menacing detachment. Behind this shark-eyed barkeep was a wall of fame, or at least of photos: a who's who of who's nude here at Tit Time. The Polaroids had been stapled to the wall with care and emblazoned with the dancers' names: Shy-anne, Pebbles, Ginger Snaps, Stormy, Misty, and Dusty. While I sat there, lost in admiration of these sirens of the runway, I was joined by the club's well-worn doorman. He offered to have me buy him a drink, or, failing that, share the one I was drinking. I declined his request for an offer, and introduced myself and my mission. He seemed excited to speak about the town he lived and worked in.

DONNIE LARSON

❧

Author's note: The following was transcribed from security-camera footage.

"Hi, my name is Donnie Larson. I work for Mr. Hollinger. I'm the manager of Tit Time Show Palace. It's the premier strip club in

Wigfield. At least that's what it says on the sign. That's what I do. I'm the manager of a strip club. Don't make me any better than the next guy.

"How would I sum up Wigfield in three words? Well, sir, that's easy.

"Number A: friendly. That's the thing about Wigfield. There's no denying it's neighborly. I see the same faces, day in and day out. It's like we're family except we're not related, we didn't grow up together, and we don't spend any time with each other. It makes you feel safe to know that if I needed a shovel or some lime, just down the road a bit is a neighbor I could take it from. Just because I don't know a lot of these people's names doesn't mean I won't ask them for things. That's the beauty of this town: neighbors who have things I want.

"Number B: slow. You cannot beat the pace of Wigfield, and I'll say that to anybody. You see, in the city, people are rushing around doing things without thinking, acting all crazy. No thank you. Here you don't have to be in a hurry to do nothing. You can take your time doing nothing and nobody pays no never mind. Sometimes I'll take twice as long to do nothing as it would take a city fella to do something just because I know I can. Last week I spent forty-five minutes putting on a sock. That's Wigfield.

"Number C: friendly people who aren't in a hurry. Now, I know that's nine words, but who's counting? Oh, are you? The point is: I couldn't imagine living anywhere else. That's the tragedy of losing a place like this; slow, friendly people with nothing to do are going to have to move somewhere else to not do it.

"That pretty much sums up Wigfield. I just think it's horrible that this town might get flooded, you know, not just for the people that might get wet, but for the industry. Through sheer will and truckers, we have built a paradise here. This town is barely a quarter mile long, and we have more gentlemen's clubs than gentlemen. We have more Pay-Per-View genitalia then Bangkok. And I know of that of which I speak of! Yes, I was in the service. Yes, I was stationed overseas. Yes, I was dishonorably discharged. And no, I don't want to talk about it. Here's what happened: I didn't know she was one of ours. I certainly didn't know she was an officer. And I meant no disrespect when I offered to treat us to her. I'm not saying I'm proud of it. Nothing to brag about. I don't think my name should be on a plaque.

"Anyway, here's the beauty of a small town. Our clubs are shoved so close together you couldn't squeeze a dead body between them, and Lord knows people have tried. Sure, we've found parts, usually had to fish them out with a coat hanger, but never a whole body. I wish I could say the same for Bangkok, which, by the way, I have got to get back to. It's a party town. Do you know what the statute of limitations is in Thailand?

"Anyway, around here a person could stumble in any direction and end up face-to-face with the tail end of some pretty fine tail. Now, cuz they're so close together, the various clubs do have their disputes, that's bound to happen, nobody's fault. But because we're a small town, these misunderstandings are settled in a small-town way, usually a knife fight, or knifing, or a slashing, or a slitting. It can get pretty entertaining sometimes. Two guys from two different clubs will be arguing over, oh, I don't know, stealing a stripper from one club and forcing her to perform in another. I know this probably sounds pretty hokey to city folk, but these two guys will square off in the street. One will pull out an old scaling knife and take a few jabs, and the other might stab back with the sharpened end of a hunting rifle. They dance around, and they get abusting and hitting against each other, then they set to screaming and then somebody'll draw a little blood, and then the guy with the rifle will plunge the barrel into the other guy's chest and pull the trigger. That's it, argument settled. We're not tied up in litigation. There are no lawyers. Nobody is thinking about justice. That's just not the small-town way.

"Here's another great thing: If you love naked women and you are, for some legal reason, restricted from driving, this is the place to be. Now, I work at Tit Time, but occasionally I get an itch to check out the competition. That's just the way I am. Everybody knows it. I can just walk to all the other clubs. I don't have to drive. I know how to drive, I mean, I got my operator's license, I just choose not to drive. I guess I'm afraid if I drive people might get hurt. And people would get hurt, that's pretty much been proven to my satisfaction. I'm not proud of it. I'll say that to anybody. I'm the first to admit that I should be nowhere near a powered vehicle. But my operator's license says different, so occasionally all hell breaks loose. I'm not asking for a medal. I wish it didn't happen, but it does, and there's not a thing in the world I can do about it."

CHAPTER THREE

A FTER Donnie's colorful onslaught of words, he offered to take me to the various other entertainment establishments Wigfield had to offer.

So, with my strip-club Sherpa guide leading the assault, we set out to scale the peaks and valleys of the town's gentlemen's clubs. We first headed over to the Bacon Strip, known locally for its midday breakfast buffet. The wait staff was both exceptionally efficient, and exceptionally nude. As I perused the various breakfast meats, I talked to Cinnamon, a dancer and twelve-year veteran of the runway who is renowned for her "salad tong" dance. We sat down in a booth as Donnie went back to the bar to add three fingers of kick to our orange juice–like beverages.

CINNAMON

"This whole thing has me up in a panic! I just don't know how people go on knowing that that water is out there just waiting to get you. What will happen to me? I mean, if they flood this town and I'm forced to leave, how am I supposed to move my mobile home? I just know in my heart of hearts that people would help us if they only knew what will be lost if this town goes away. People can't help what they don't know. I can't help the starving people of India, because I don't know what they need. But I would help if I did, and so would other people. If there is one thing I've learned working in the adult section of the sex industry, it's that people are basically friendly. I think people's first impression of Wigfield is that it is just a chain of porno shops, strip clubs, and used auto parts yards. Well, it's a lot more than that. It's pornographers and strippers and people who sell used auto parts. And these people have lives. It's our lives that are going to be lost.

"I can't stand the idea that this place might disappear. I just think it's sad that one day there might come a day when a small-town girl like me won't have a place she can take her clothes off in front of truckers.

"What I do to get through my day is stick to my routine, and I don't let myself get diverted. I have a simple philosophy: KOKO! Which stands for Keep On Keepin' On. You know? Keep on living, even if it kills you. From the outside you might think my life looks pretty sad, I mean, people are missing, people I know are missing, parts of people I know are missing, but you just have to stay positive. You know, KOKO! You just have to learn lessons in life. If you get burned by your stove, don't keep touching it, get rid of it! Now, I know my days must sound pretty plain or simple to someone from the city, but it keeps me busy.

"I keep a diary. I been keepin' a diary since I was fourteen years old. Writing in a diary is like a muscle, you have to do it every day or you could easily pull it. Even if I don't have anything to say, I write: 'Dear diary, I don't have anything to say today, maybe tomorrow.' Sometimes I get tired of writing the same thing, so instead I might write: 'Dear diary, nothing coming today, I'll see you tomorrow.' The point is to write every day."

Author's note: Something about this revelation stopped me dead in my tracks like a freight train stopping dead on its tracks.* It occurred to me that a lot of talking was going on, but what about this diary? As a fellow diarist, journalist, and literary-ist, I asked to take a look at this most personal document to first peruse, praise, and then Xerox so that I might include it in this book. Here is an excerpt:

9:15 a.m.

Awakened by nightmare of squealing babies and barking dogs. So tired . . .

10:30 a.m.

Suddenly rousted . . . reoccurring nightmare . . . babies screaming, dogs howling . . . must sleep . . .

---

*Note to self: Remember to freshen up train metaphor before book goes to print! Other metaphor ideas: Plane stopping dead in its tracks? Boat, bicycle, dirigible, human cannonball, hitchhiker, rickshaw?†

† Note: Remember to order Chinese food, no MSG. Headaches!!!!

12:00 p.m.

Awakened again by the sound of barking dogs and squealing babies. After feeding the dogs and the babies, it's on with the gym shoes and shorts and then back into bed for a quick nap.

12:45 p.m.

I'm up and this time it might take. I hitch a ride over to the abandoned gas tower, where I run the only stairs in town—211 stairs up, 74 down—for eight breathless minutes. I must show time who's boss.

1:30 p.m.

I head over to Mumpson Used Tires where I have an unpaid internship. I'm trying to break into the business, prepare for my future. I don't think there is any denying that used tires will always be a big seller. My boss, Junior Mumpson Sr., says, "The only tire that is never tired is a Mumpson's used tire." I don't know what that means, but I stand by it. During work, I talk to Cooter on the phone. He keeps paging me about a bachelor party he wants me to work. I ask him the big three questions: How many guys? What's the pay? Do they know I'm an albino? Because I'm at work, I talk quietly so my voice is muffled. Everyone here knows I'm a stripper, but it seems right to pretend I'm being secretive.

5:30 p.m.

I head over to The Bacon Strip. I'm wearing the usual one-piece nylon dress-itard. It's easy to slip off, and it doesn't hold an odor. It really is a miracle fabric. I'm feeling good because tonight is my night to dance in the barrel. I do private shows inside an oil drum for twenty bucks a pop. One guy tries to touch me and I quickly tell him the rules. Customers are not allowed to touch the dancers with their hands. For a twenty-dollar tip, I'll caress my breast and ass while they jerk off on my shoulder, or for another ten, they can buy a pokin' rod. It's a pretty good night. I have a lot of customers, and they almost all purchased rods. Men love barrel dances. Sometimes I think I should invest in my own oil drum, but I don't really have a head for numbers.

12:30 a.m.

There are about twelve guys at the bachelor party. They are pretty lit by the time I show up. I do my usual routine: remove all my clothes, work the two-headed dildo, urinate into a punch bowl, and shoot hush puppies from my vagina, but because I'm tired, I skip the card tricks. Most of the guys are pretty friendly, and they seem mostly satisfied, but one guy calls me Rabbit Eyes, which gets a pretty big laugh until Cooter breaks his skull with the thick side of a broken pool cue. That gets a bigger laugh. Cooter collects sixty bucks while I pass out business cards and then on the couch.

4:45 a.m.

I'm finally back home. I'm sixty bucks lighter than I expected to be. Cooter told me I spent the money on drugs, but I don't feel high. I can't wait to get into my hammock. It takes awhile to get the babies and the dogs down, but there's nothing like a little warmed caramel to shut them up. I gaze out the window. I watch the trucks whiz by on the freeway. The sound always reminds me of a tiny country stream with giant trucks roaring down it. I think how lucky I am to live here. Then I pop two Darvon and let the sweet darkness cover me.

FOUR

CHAPTER FOUR

Author's note: The following comes to you live via the tape recorder that I just received from my editor at Hyperion, who seems to think I don't type legibly enough.

DAWN, or noon, it doesn't really matter. What does matter is that the pinpoints of sunlight that have found their way through the weave of the heavy woolen blanket pulled tightly over my head are like lasers etching a litany of pain onto the rear interior of my skull. What day is it? According to the notch marks in the Grimmetts' guest bedroom wall, I've been in Wigfield for nine days. Nine days! If my calculations are correct, that would mean the nine days would break down thusly: Day one, pulled into town, set up shop, met residents. Days two through eight, these seem a little hazy. If I remember accurately, and I don't, it seems that I have spent the time in the presence of a certain town member engaged in a drinking-slash-strip-club research binge.

For those of you who don't write, it needs to be explained that research is an essential element of the writing process. And occasionally, in-depth research requires one to get one's hands dirty. I think I can say with confidence that my hands are filthy. I must admit, those eight days of exploration have taken their toll. I'm having trouble recalling the title of the book. I barely remember the topic. I roll out of my cot and furiously reread my contract. Yep, this proves it, I have a book to write. It wasn't some horrible nightmare. I plow through my notes, scattered about the room like wind-driven leaves, looking for a clue, a hint of theme, anything that might set me back on the path. Nothing. Just a wild mishmash of conflicting information. If only I had something to go on other than my own writing. Stupid! Stupid! I begin to search my dresser for my clothes until I realize I left them hanging on my body. For the first time since I began this undertaking, a serious hurdle, other than the archaic laws regarding copyright, has been set between me and the finish line. I am sick. My skull aches as if pygmies are pounding out a rhythmic jungle beat on that spot where my eyeballs attach to their nerves. In hindsight, I should have been able to look back at my behavior and project into the future with 20/20 vision that I was heading for a meltdown. One cannot give the kind of dedication I have given to this project and not expect to blow off a little steam, like a safety valve that keeps my artistic boiler from exploding. I guess the real blame lies at the feet of my coldhearted, unfeeling editor who obviously has no qualms about working me like a sharecropper.

I stumble blindly like a hungover bear to find the Grimmetts sitting at their kitchen table having a bite to eat. They bid me a good afternoon and then ask how the book is going. Good question, I think. I wonder what the answer is. Luckily I have made a lot of easy promises to a lot of angry people, and it isn't long before one of them is knocking on the Grimmetts' door.

Into the house steps a tiny man, no bigger than an enormous dwarf. The police uniform he sports might cause fear in some, but I know that I have nothing to worry about. Not in this state anyway. He tells me his name is Hoyt Gein, one of the police chiefs, and he is here to make his statement for the book I am writing about Wigfield and the dam coming down. Ahhhh, back on track. He invites himself onto the screened-in porch, where I listen while applying a cold compress to my eye sockets, and he paces like a caged ferret.

HOYT GEIN

"I'm the police chief under Charles Halstead, who is the legitimately self-declared mayor of Wigfield. Understand? Now, you might run into a couple of other fellas around town, shooting off their mouths claiming to be mayor, but my man is the real deal. If he wasn't, then how could I be the chief of police? Think about it: I haven't. 'Cause I don't have to, 'cause I know he is the mayor. See what I mean? Now, I also want to dispel any rumors you might have heard that Mayor Halstead is my puppet, and that he's not competent to run a third of this town. Well, that accusation is just laughable and amusing. Now, while I may have encouraged him to run, and it is true that I'm his strongest supporter, and just because I help him dress himself doesn't mean the man is not fit to hold office. Have I cleared that up? I know some of the townspeople, namely Fleet Hollinger, have criticized Mayor Halstead for having me have him appoint me chief of police, given my arson arrest record, but come on now, that's just ludicrous. I can stop lighting fires anytime I want. End of story. Did I shine enough of a light on that for you? Yes, I occasionally start fires when I'm out at a social event, but so what? Who doesn't? It's a free country. I have complete control over my desire to unleash the flickering golden god.

"Can we move on now, or would you rather spend the rest of our time dwelling on these false rumors? Go ahead, keep firing off these accusations, I'll just keep knockin' them out of the park. See, I'm no stranger to an ambush. I came prepared. So maybe if you're done with your sneak attack, we could move on to something more relevant. Unless you want to keep going around in circles, which is fine with me, 'cause I brought my dancing shoes.

"How 'bout we talk about the town. This is a good town, but we got some problems to solve. That's well known. The truth is, life was simpler when we didn't have public officials and I was the only security personnel. But things change. Fires get lit, a building gets destroyed, blame gets laid, people get fired, and vendettas get started. What do you know, we're here again, more allegations about me setting people on fire. Isn't it funny how that happens? If this is the pond you want to go skinny dipping in, fine, I know how to swim. I can dog-paddle all day. I've got nothing to do. I'm the police chief. Look, why don't I just give this baby a bottle and put it to bed. All right, any objections?

"Fleet Hollinger thought he could force me out and appoint himself mayor, but this is America, that's not the way it works. Then you know what he does? He thinks, hell, he'll hold an election, and just because he's the most powerful man in town, he'll get elected. Well, that's not the way things work either. A curious electrical fire at the polling station saw to that. It turns out it's pretty hard to exercise your right to vote when you're on fire. Case closed. In the confusion, the town ended up with three mayors. Maybe that's not an ideal situation, but that's what happens when I feel threatened. There, you happy? Now maybe you can give that finger of yours a rest, unless you got your heart set on pointing it at me. I don't have time to waste on this nonsense. I have more important matters to talk about, but maybe that's not gonna sell books, in which case I apologize. Now maybe we can talk about the town?

"I do things a little different here. It's all part of being a small-town sheriff. I have small-town concerns. Maybe saving a little town like Wigfield isn't important to most people, but it's important to me. I

know most people don't cotton to small towns. Like lemmings, they
follow everyone else to the cities, where they can find jobs, housing,
and culture. Well, I guess our priorities are a little different here.
What's important to us can't be categorized in a list. It can't be
written down or even expressed verbally. It's locked away in our
hearts and settled in our arteries. In Wigfield's parade, the drum we
march to is the beat of our hearts. You scrape away the
unemployment, the unsolved murders, or even the contaminated
topsoil, and what you'll find is the giant swollen heart of America.

"The first thing we as a town have to do is get our priorities straight
and clean up this place, or we will never get the tourist trade back.
Top of my list is to find out who's killing all these people. I have
already narrowed down the list of Mr. or Mrs. Murderer or Murderers.
The second first thing we need to do is establish a profile of the perp.
Now, my investigation has shown that the victims were killed by a
blunt trauma to the back of the head or stabbing or shooting or
poisoning or burning or . . . did I say shooting? This is often followed
by dismemberment. Or preceded. It's really hard to tell after a while.
But clearly this is a person who is a local and familiar to everyone or a
stranger just passing through whose movements remain a mystery.
Another pattern is that the murders occur at night with the exception
of those that happen in the daytime with the sole exception to that
exception being the string of dusk and dawn killings.

"Point is, we're going to get him/her/it. It only stands to reason.
With all the police chiefs in town the odds are in our favor. It works
out that for every twelve people we have a police chief, excluding the
other police chiefs, who I wouldn't protect even if I was paid to,
which I am. We can't tackle crime in this city until we can figure out
who is the rightful police chief. This sometimes leads to arguments
which are usually solved by ramming another police chief's vehicle
into the side of the arsenic runoff containment tank, causing a
magnificent, hypnotizing blaze in which the joyful flames rise and
dance in celebration of my victory! Now there you go again. How do
we always end up right back were we started? Ring around a rosy,

pocket full of posie. At this point, I'm not even angry; frankly, I'm just getting bored with this merry-go-round of baseless claims, which, I gotta say, is making me feel pretty angry and maybe even a little threatened, and that's something I think we both can agree nobody wants. Maybe it would be best for all involved if we wrap this up before things combust. It is a waste of my time and the town's money for me to sit here and be forced to defend myself against ridiculous assertions.

"So I'll just make a quick comment about the dam and then I'm done. Got it? Here goes. I don't think they should tear down the dam. There you go. Is that simple enough for you to understand? Don't tear it down. Why would I want to see my town destroyed? Besides, if they tear down the dam and the water comes rushing forth, what will become of my children—the flames? The thought of them struggling bravely against the rising tide makes me want to lash out, or rather unleash their wrath against those who would attempt to destroy them."

And then, as if to prove a point, after Hoyt finished with his statement, he demanded that I follow him out to his camper van. Any doubt I had as to his official capacity was dispelled by the words *Wigfield's Police Chief* stenciled on the side of his customized Vanagon. Throwing open the rear cargo door with a flourish, he proudly displayed a man in his early forties who was elaborately seat-belted into a lawn chair. According to Hoyt, this cheerfully disheveled man was Mayor Charles Halstead, who had insisted on meeting me. We lifted His Honor out of the cargo bay and placed him on a sunny patch of gravel. Of course I was honored to meet my first mayor.

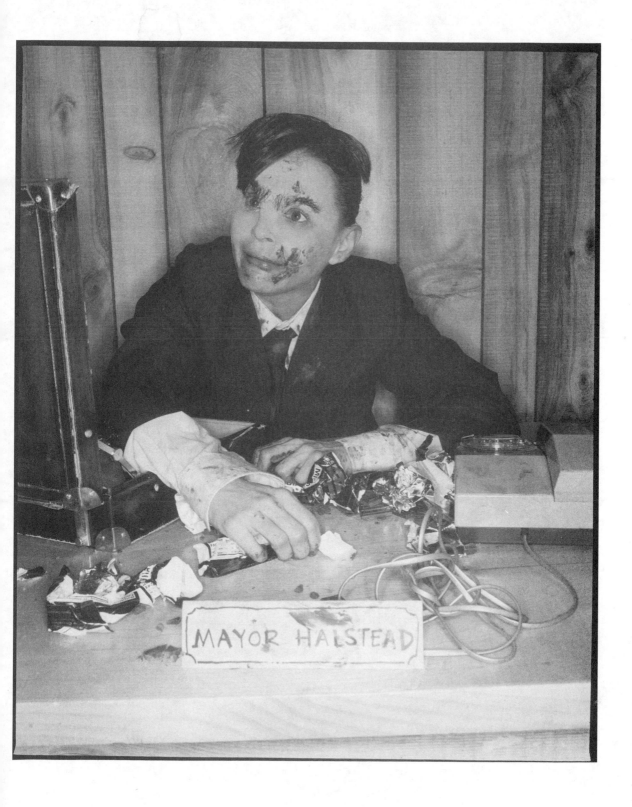

CHARLES HALSTEAD

"I like fudge. It's chocolaty, and it's sweet. It feels good in my mouth but it makes me thirsty. I like being a lawyer. It makes me proud. I have a briefcase. I keep my fudge in there. You can have some if you want. Not too much though. It will make you thirsty. I'm not from here, but I live here now. I came to this town to represent the lead dispersal plant. The government wanted to close it because they said it was retarding the employees. So they closed it. I got a court order that allowed me to stay at the plant so I could disprove firsthand the effects of the plant. I like watches; they're shiny. They make a ticktock sound that tickles my ears. Have you seen my wife? After I lost the case, I decided to stay in Wigfield. I don't know why. When my wife would come to visit me, she used to cry and try to explain something to me, but I can't remember what. I like fudge. Guess what I have in my briefcase. I'm one of the mayors. I hope they don't tear down the dam. My fudge would get wet."

CHAPTER FIVE

ALTHOUGH his honor's political agenda seemed a bit unfocused and oddly fudge-centric, it was clear that there was some infrastructure to this town, a local political body that could battle against the tyrannical incursions of the antidam forces. I knew now that a vital part of this story was the mayor. All three of him. I had met one, but I knew that some more of them were out there somewhere, and I aimed to go where them some were.

This search quickly led me to the business establishment of Mayor Burchal Sawyer. We met in his vast junkyard. Cars were stacked in rows and stretched for as far as my eye would look, like giant rusted metal corn with wheels. My meeting with him served two purposes: First, it would afford me an interview with another of the three mayors of this town. Second, I still needed an alternator, which I miraculously found in a car that was nearly identical to the one I abandoned by the highway, even down to the all my stuff in the trunk.

Burchal Sawyer is a commanding figure who exudes an air of leadership and a thick layer of sweat. A man of indeterminate age, his hunched posture had a nobility that befit his mayoral stature. As I pulled the exact engine part

I needed from the car that so closely resembled my own, Burchal regaled me with a pleasant yarn.

BURCHAL SAWYER

❧

"I've been shit kickin' around this county for more years than a Chink's got rice. I've moved from one town to the other, never really staying in any one place longer than it would take someone to get a restraining order, but I knew, the moment I laid my fingers on this place, I wasn't leavin' and I'm not. You hear that, Fleet Hollinger? The next time he opens that cock holster he calls a mouth I'm gonna slap his head off his shoulders. And I'll goddamn do it, too. See how it works? I'm the great American success story. One day you're livin' out of your car, the next you're livin' out of your car, and you're the mayor of a town. I practically run this place, and I'm not even fully unpacked. That's because I make things happen.

"Let me tell you how I did it. When I came to this town, the first thing that caught my eye was the huge number of abandoned cars. I had never seen such a glorious crop ready to be harvested. Wigfield's greatest natural resource is the rusted chassis. I hauled all them cars into a pile, built a fence around it, and presto! I'm the operator of the largest junkyard in Wigfield. You can't argue with that kind of success, unless you're Fleet Hollinger. The point is, he's got me to deal with now, and that's just the way it is. I'm not going away. I'm not gonna vaporize. Nobody is gonna find my bones in a storm drain so that they gotta identify me by my dental records. Okay? That's not gonna happen.

"This is the way it's gonna go: When the state tears down the dam and we get that relocation money, I'm getting my share because I'm

one third of the municipal government and none of Fleet's threats about sending his boy Lenare over to cut me open like a trout is going to change that. Do you see a hook in my mouth? Wait a minute, why are you asking all these questions? You working for Hollinger? Just tell me now, cuz if I find out later you work for Hollinger, they're gonna find your bones in a storm drain. You got me?

"Let me tell you something about this town: In the land of the blind, Fleet Hollinger is nothing but a nigger-lovin' faggot, and I don't mean any disrespect to Afro-American black people or . . . uh . . . uh . . . faggots. Hey, you want to hear a joke? Listen to this. Hollinger tried to tell me that I couldn't run for mayor of this town because I didn't have a residence. I was livin' in my car at the time. Just because a man doesn't have a place to shit, doesn't mean he won't. Then he gets his balls in a bunch just 'cause I didn't have any identification. I know who I am. I don't need fingerprints to prove it. It was a curling wand accident. Plus, he says that I'm not educated, and that's a crock of shit. Look, last time I checked this was a free country.

"Now, a lot of people ask me how I acquired so many abandoned cars in such a small community. Well, the answer is simple. It's none of their goddamn business. And I resent the implication that I am murdering people for their cars, if that is indeed what they are implying, which would make perfect sense because, let's face it, how am I getting all these cars? I just want this community to rest assured that there are probably plenty of ways to get around killing people for their cars. Here's one: Unattended cars will be towed. If it's not claimed within a reasonable period of time, technically, it's mine. That's the one bit of law that I'm most proud of pushin' through. You see, as one of the mayors here, I can introduce rules into the community that will benefit everybody, starting with me. It's what in government we call the dribble-down effect. I guess this can best be illustrated by imagining Wigfield as a human being. Now, the head, which would be me, is the leader of the community, which is the body. Make sense? When I feed myself, or the head, some of the food is bound to dribble down my chin and gather in my facial hair. The rest of the town gets to feed off all the tasty morsels that are crusting in my beard. If I don't put food in my mouth, then there are no crumbs for anybody else. What kind of mayor would I be if I was keeping crumbs from the public's mouths? I don't see Fleet Hollinger throwin' 'em any crumbs. You follow? See, you've got to understand that even in a small town, the head needs to remain strong in order for the body to survive. This town deserves for me to be the head. I'm willing to fight to keep that alive in this town, at least until the dam comes down and destroys it.

"Speaking of which, as one of the mayors, I feel I should chime in about this dam business. On the record, my official reaction is this: Why would the state want to tear our dam down? It just doesn't make any sense: flooding a riverbed? What kind of logic is that? But if they say they gotta do it, well then, who am I to argue? Do you think I want to lose my town? You think just because I'm used to livin' in my car it will be easy for me to pull up stakes and drive to another place? But again, I repeat, if it's got to come down, well then, I say, as a community we prepare ourselves for the horrifying loss we must endure, and on behalf of the town I accept my money graciously."

CHAPTER SIX

THIS left only Fleet to complete the trifecta of local leadership. But where would I find him? Logic said his home. Locals told me to try him at home. But I had to go with my gut, which led me to his house.

The phrase "sprawling ramshackle compound" is thrown around all too casually these days, but in this case it is the only way to describe the Hollinger residence. Clearly Fleet did not want for land, merely planning. A series of double- and singlewide trailers had been hauled into an impressive maze of aluminum and connected in a haphazard fashion with sheet metal and button rivets. More than anything else, it gave the impression of a giant human Habitrail. Clearly this was the home of an important man.

Surrounding all this was a high barbed-wire fence, inside of which stood a cadre of snarling canines. But following the old adage that a snarling dog never bites, I scaled the fence, dropped to the ground, and enjoyed a brief mauling. I quickly occupied the dog's snapping jaws with my limbs to buy some time until I could figure out what to do with all this pain. I might have gone from worst to wurst if it had not been for the timely intercession of a protective angel.

She pulled the dogs off me with a light whistle, a simple hand command,

and a few vicious kicks to their ribs. Hustling me through the front door before the beasts regrouped, she checked me for puncture wounds then retreated to a far easy chair and pulled a bolster pillow onto her lap. In the stifling silence of the dark, paneled den, this Mother Teresa in a tube top stared at me through a tangle of bangs. I broke from her disquieting gaze and looked about the small squat room. Pictures of the girl hung on every wall, as if this were a shrine to some pale adolescent saint. I asked her name, and she said it was Carla. Her dad wasn't home; she's not supposed to have strangers in the house; would I please leave? I found her directness refreshing, her forthrightness appealing, and her dogs terrifying. I insisted that I stay and interview her for the book.

CARLA PORT HOLLINGER

"Sorry about the dogs. My dad says they only attack in the presence of people.

"I know you came to talk to my dad, but if you really want to, you can talk to me. I mean, I don't know why anyone would want to talk to me. They've never talked to me before. Besides, I don't really have anything to say. I mean, I'm pretty ordinary. I come from an ordinary family. My dad's one of the mayors, my parents split up, and now my mom is some kind of lesbian witch.

"Why do I run away so much? I don't know. I guess to get out of here. Not that I want to go anywhere. I'm sure to an outsider this looks like a pretty nice town. But it's kinda boring, and there's not a lot to do, but it keeps us pretty busy.

"I go to school up in Shell Knob. We're not part of the district or anything. We just stand up by the highway where the bus comes by and most days they pick us up. I like school. We used to all go there together. Me and Regina and Judy and . . . Dillard. But we haven't been going to school that much this last semester. They changed the bus route, and we can't find it.

"What else can I say about the town? It gets pretty hot in the summer. But it's nice to have seasons. I wish we had 'em. And of course there're those stories about the Wigfield Maniac, how there's a madman in town, but I don't believe it's real. I think somebody is killing folks just to scare people.

"I suppose the big news now is that they might tear the dam down. I don't know how I feel about that. I guess it's horrible that the town might disappear. We used to go up to the top of the dam and drink malt coolers. Me and Regina and . . . Dillard. That was pretty fun . . . until Dillard wrote that horrible thing on the dam. And it's not true either. I don't see how they could have. I was there almost all the time.

"I don't care if the dam comes down or if we're considered a town or anything. I'm just seventeen. I've lived in Wigfield my whole life, but it might be longer. Sometimes I feel like this entire town is the Maniac, slowly tightening a cord around my neck just to watch all the colors I'm turning. I couldn't imagine living anywhere else.

"I belong to a poetry club, well it was me and Regina but she's not in it anymore, so it's just me now. Anyway, I wrote this poem about the dam and everything. They might print it in the *Wigfield Sporadic*.

"PLEASE, WATER, HEAR MY PLEAS

"Oh please, Water, hear my pleas . . .

Water dark green water

Don't carry my parents away

Smashing their hollow lives against the rocks

Bashing them again and again

Relentless and merciless

Until their bones are stripped of flesh

And bob like driftwood on your roaring currents.

"And please, Water, while you're not at it . . .

Don't sweep away my brother

Your mighty flow taking him to be

Never heard from again.

"And don't make him suffer

By holding him under for long periods of time,

But not enough to kill him.

Please don't let him resurface occasionally

To taste the sweet air of life

Only to be dragged back into the murky depths.

"And Water, when you don't do this

Don't let his ankle hook on a log

So only his eyes clear the surface

While you rush into his nose and throat

Filling his lungs with your dark green liquidness.

"Water, hear my pleas . . .

Don't wash away my family

I could not bear to be the object of sympathy

To have Dillard Rankin say,

'She's the one who lost her family.

I feel so bad for her

I want to hold her

I want to comfort her.'

I couldn't stomach the jealous stares

Of Regina Cox as her boyfriend Dillard, the one she

Stole from me, has his arms wrapped tightly around my waist

Planting gentle kisses on my neck.

Comforting me . . . comforting me . . .

O Lord, watch out for the wave, Regina . . .

Please don't die horribly with the last thing you

Ever see is me being kissed by Dillard Rankin.

"Please, Water, hear my pleas."

After speaking to Carla, I realized something mysterious was happening to my story. Something new and natural and exciting yet somehow dangerous and forbidden. Yes, like a young teenager standing in the foyer of Womanhood, so was the story of Wigfield ready to blossom. Its secrets thrust into the open like budding breasts. Its structure maturing so quickly that it grows awkward and gangly yet undeniably alluring. This very story's reluctance to emerge is perhaps what makes it so tempting to coax the transition along. I felt I had so much to teach this story, if only it would trust me. I could usher this story into an adult world of pleasure. Yes, the story is scared and naive, that's why it needs to be massaged and gently prodded under my firm tutelage.

But what if someone found out? I pondered this question as I took leave of Carla and went in search of her father.

CHAPTER SEVEN

WHILE looking for Fleet, I suddenly realized I had some urgent business to attend to first. Mother Nature came a callin', and this time I intended to be a gracious host. Normally, in lieu of a loo, I'd seek refuge in the semiprivacy of the nearest alley and do my dirty business upon the masonry. Today, however, I decided to seek out a proper public rest room.

I include this personal account of my bodily functions, because, on this occasion, it led me to one of the many colorful characters living in Wigfield. Running short on time, and long on bloat, I stumbled upon a charming wooden structure with a tin roof. Although it was a bit larger than the previous outhouses I had christened with my humors, it was immediately recognizable. Upon entering, I was taken aback at the care given to liven up this place of relievement. The walls were covered in lifelike dead animals as if herds of curious beasts had poked their heads through the many portholes of this pissoir like so many furry voyeurs, intent on catching a forbidden glimpse of a half-naked patron in this public chamber pot. But where were the urinals? Then it struck me, this was no ordinary outhouse, the furnishings were a clear indication of that. And then I realized, in keeping with the wildlife theme, along the wall, at waist level, were the open waiting maws of animal heads that were obviously inventive covers for the plumbing fixtures. I decided to acquaint myself with the nearest wild boar. While I favored the beast with a liberal dose of my home brew, I mused on the difference between city and small-town life. In the big city it costs you a quarter to stand at a cold porcelain receptacle, but here in Wigfield, free of charge, they turn even the most mundane activities into a carnival of arts and crafts. I couldn't wait to return after my next hefty meal and feed the bobcat. Suddenly a loud pounding emanated from outside. I quickly responded with the customary, "Occupado." The knocking didn't cease, but grew louder, now matched with shouts of incoherent fury. Clearly, this next customer was either ignorant of outhouse etiquette or his bowels were. Luckily I had thrown the dead bolt. I quickly finished my urinary agenda and crossed to unlatch the door and perhaps give my friend with the impatient colon a firm little piece of my mind.

The Guinness Book of World Records states that the longest single feat of holding one's breath is nine minutes and eighteen seconds. It is said that a well-conditioned South Seas pearl diver can stay under water on a single lungful of air for nearly six minutes. My own experience, however, tells me that a deep feeling of panic grips the mind about eight seconds in, and at the half-minute mark—about the time it took for me to pry his hands from around my neck—Death looms over you like a sadistic cousin at a family picnic.

It seems that I had in fact stumbled into the taxidermy shop of one Lenare Degroat. When he found that the door had been locked on what he referred to as his Stuffin' Shed, he became alarmed, and then alarming. From the comfort of the floor, I calmly explained to his fist that I had merely taken a wrong turn, that I was a journalist trying to capture the spirit of this heroic settlement as it battled against the indifferent governmental apparati. I requested an interview, which he granted with a grunt. While he spoke candidly, I listened guardedly, strategically placing myself between Degroat and the soggy boar's head, which now drooped lazily as if narcotized by my recent offering.

LENARE

"I'm the taxidermist here in town. The people 'round here have a little joke about me. They say, 'Don't cross Lenare, or he'll slice you open, scoop out your innards, fill you with sawdust, and then mount you.' I guess it's more of a warning than a joke. I don't like to be crossed. I guess that's why I ended up doing what I do. It's not that I feel a sense of power when I poke out an animal's eye and replace it with a glass marble, it's that I feel domination. Animals think they are so superior to us. They pretend to act innocent, all furry and frolicsome, but when we're not looking, they mock us. As I cut away the skin from a deer's skull, I always think, 'Who's laughing now?' Usually it's me. Most folks in the big city don't understand nature. They live in their concrete buildings, on their concrete streets, fucking their concrete wives. They are not around trees and rocks, who taunt them all the time. Well, maybe a place like this doesn't mean much to city folk, but it means something to us, even if the squirrels make sport of me behind my back.

"There is no better place on earth for hunting than right here in

Wigfield. I like to go out with my buddies early in the morning. We got all the gear: camo fatigues, face paint, high-powered rifles. We don't wear any of that pussy crap like orange vests, you know, so the other hunter won't shoot you? Well, that just takes all the sport out of it, don't it? And I'm tired of hearing all that bullshit from those East Coast college-educated liberal types who have their yarmulkes in a bind because they think animals need to be protected. That's just a load of crap. Did you know a chimpanzee is capable of rape? Capable, hell, it's likely! If I still had the ability to conceive a child, I wouldn't let my daughter near one of those furry bastards. Most animals are just waiting for their chance to take a swipe at a human. It's in their nature. They're animals, that's why we call them that. They don't have souls. They have nothing to fear in the afterlife. They have nothing to lose! A hummingbird would gladly peck your eyes out. It would amuse it. It would hover above your eye socket sucking out your eye juice like nectar and throw it back up to its waiting hungry children! I'm not making this stuff up, I'm imagining it. They're just waiting for us to let our guard down. That's why we've got to go on the offensive.

"Of course, one of the nice things about Wigfield is a lot of the time you can go out hunting with just a basket. I just scoop the critters right off the steamy ground and shake them a bit to make sure they're dead. I can't wait to get them back to my Stuffin' Shed.

"People from the city travel miles to get to places like Wigfield. A quiet, rural place where they can relax and kill animals, and now the government wants to flood the place. It just doesn't make any sense. Sometimes I think about declaring open hunting season on that Representative Farber. I would love to track him into the woods, following his scent. I can smell fear. I feed on it! As I'd close in on him, I would hear his panicked breathing, his unsure footing snapping twigs as fatigue sets in. I'd get him on the run and try to force him into an open field. Then, from about a hundred yards, I'd drop him with a leg shot. He'd writhe in the dirt, yelping. I'd close in on him until I was standing over him, tears in his eyes, trembling. Then I'd squeeze off another round. Don't get me wrong. I don't have any ill will toward anybody, except for maybe the people . . . yeah, the people.

"Let me just put in a word here about something that I find offensive. Freeze-drying. Now, if you don't know what I'm talking about, I'll try to describe it without losing my lunch. What some so-called taxidermists are doing these days is instead of slicing an animal open, yanking out the innards, deboning and tossing the skin on the fleshing wheel to scrape off the excess fat and sebum before it goes rancid on you—damn, that wheel can do a job on an animal—they . . . they take the same animal, pose it in some natural way, then pop it into the freeze dryer. Abraca-daisy, you get your animal back. Where is the satisfaction in that? These aren't our buddies. This is an opponent who needs to be taught the lesson that you only hinted at when you killed it. And if you don't follow through with the dismemberment, what sort of message are you sending his filthy, furry friends?

"Let me just say one more thing here. I am offended by the term *lifelike*. Take a look at what I do. You'd never mistake these animals for alive. Hell, when I'm done, they barely look like animals. And another thing: naturalistic poses. Frolicking in some moss. Holding a nut. What's the point of that? If you wanted this squirrel to hold a nut, then why did you lock yourself in mortal combat with it? That's why I like to capture that last moment before the animal gives up the ghost. You can almost feel the fear rising off it like a stink. I don't coddle my dead animals.

"But I try not to get too worked up about it. This taxidermy thing is just a hobby. My real job is over at the morgue.

"Hollinger's morgue. We're a full-service morgue. A person couldn't pick a better place to leave a stiff. We're not only a storage facility/incinerator, we also prepare the body for burial/incineration. One of the things I do over there is to make sure that all the bodies that come in are dead. Here's my test: I just do things to them that no living human would allow, and if they don't react, then I know they're dead. And if they do react, well, the severity of the test usually makes that moot. A lot of people have a fear of being buried alive. But I am here to tell you that if you ever have the good fortune to pass through Hollinger's place, you may not be dead when you come in, but you'll be dead when you leave. You can bank on it."

CHAPTER EIGHT

TWO things became clear after speaking to Lenare Degroat: One, steer clear of Lenare Degroat, and two, the name Fleet Hollinger kept bobbing to the top of conversations like a corpse in a creek. I must find Fleet! I decided to head over to Hollinger's morgue in hopes of a chance meeting with the infamously unknown business leader. Walking down the street, I noticed how oppressively hot the town seemed. Looking down, I saw my shoes were melting into the asphalt as if they were Fudgesicles. The situation quickly went from intriguing to agonizing. I began to hop from one foot to the other on the hot asphalt like a Russian Cossack dancer on hot asphalt. My attempts to maintain my composure in front of the few locals wandering the area were thrown over and replaced by my attempts to save my feet. My attention was momentarily drawn to a piercing scream. A high-pitched bone-rattling scream. My God, what kind of brutal beating was being administered to that small child, or perhaps a helpless animal was having the life squeezed out of it? Although I couldn't definitely identify its source, one thing was certain, it was a hopeless cry, a mournful cry, a cry to break one's heart, and it sounded an awful lot like me. My pain forced my focus to return to my feet, which now were parboiled in my socks, steamed by my own juices like the mysterious meatlike products inside a tamale. In the distance, I spied a morgue. I made a dash for its cool shadows.

After waiting a few minutes for the rubber on my shoes to reset, I began to investigate the morgue. On first impression, the place resembled Count Dracula's castle if Count Dracula's castle had drop tile ceilings, linoleum floors, and fluorescent lighting. The far wall was lined with huge, unmarked metal drawers, as if some giant had installed a filing cabinet to alphabetize his deceased. I called out for Fleet Hollinger but got no response. Then I noticed a single steel table in the center of the room that appeared to have an occupant. I swallowed deeply and approached. There upon the cold metal counter lay the hideous shriveled remains of some poor old woman. How long had she been here? It must have been days. Why hadn't they embalmed her? Her skin was leathery and as gnarled as a walnut shell. Her brittle hair clung to her skull like the whiskers on a coconut. Somehow all her vital juices had been drained from her body, leaving a withered husk of a human, a bag of bones topped by a skull so small it looked like a cannibal's shrunken lodge-pole totem or perhaps a cheap plastic sideshow trinket.

And then it spoke.

"Hello. Didn't hear you come in. Give me a hand up."

After my initial shock and the series of aftershocks that followed, I tentatively reached my hand out and helped her into a sitting position.

"That's a dear. Just taking a little catnap. Sometimes when the heat gets unbearable, I like to make my way in here. They keep it pretty cool."

I explained to her my mission.

MAE ELLA PADGETT

"Oh, you'll never find Fleet down here. He leaves all this business to Lenare's handy hands.

"Besides, if you really want to know about Wigfield, you don't need Fleet. You need me! I'm the oldest resident in town. I'm like a celebrity! Whenever people see me they say, 'There goes Mae Ella, the oldest person in town!' Well, I don't know to what or to whom I have to thank for my forty-eight years on this earth, but I hope the old ticker just keeps on tickin'! I guess you could say I'm the town historian. I've spent every one of my forty-eight years right here in Wigfield, except for the times I've been incarcerated or living elsewhere. But even during my stay at the women's prison up in Shell Knob I managed to get news about the town. I'd talk to girls in the yard or in the mess. It's a funny thing about Shell Knob state confinatentuary, when you look out into the yard, you see so many of the ladies from Wigfield, you would swear you were at one of the town picnics! I suppose the only difference is, in Wigfield we don't have armed guards on top of our electrified fences, although Lord knows we could've used 'em a few times. Nothing restores order to a rioting mob quite like a hail of random gunfire.

"I guess the worst part of prison was the loneliness. You had to find ways to entertain yourself. Sometimes I would have long conversations with the lady in the mirror. One time she confessed to being the Wigfield Maniac, but I didn't believe her.

"In all my years, I guess I can say one thing for certain about Wigfield: It's a simple town! We have one currency exchange, Snyder's Esso, just outside of town; let's see . . . four adult bookstores, two with booths; eleven used auto parts, four specializing in tires; sixteen gentlemen's clubs; three morgues; and an old movie house that is now either a gentlemen's club or a morgue, I forget which. I know some

outsiders might say we have more than our share of gentlemen's clubs; well, that may be true. I'm not saying I approve. I've been around; I know what's going on. I spent a little time in Java briefly dabbling in the escort trade. Me and my compadres would sneak into some small village, collect a whole bunch of girls, and take them across the river on a cattle barge. We'd throw them scraps of meat—chicken and such—and watch them fight over it on the deck. The strong ones we'd make into working girls; the weak ones we'd send into the cane fields. One time these pirates boarded our vessel. They tried to drill me for information. They took three of my toes, two of which were never returned. Anyway, once we docked on the other side, we'd crop the girls' hair short to get rid of the lice. They'd work for a couple of weeks, and then the people from social services would come and take them back to their village, and then we'd have to go capture them all over again. Sometimes we'd take a finger just to teach them a lesson, but never the thumb. Did you know the opposable thumb is a vital part of the profession? Can't give a hand job without one. That's why raccoons are so valuable. Anyway, one time we ran out of girls so we tried to capture some orangutans to service the German and Japanese businessmen. I guess the point is I miss the days of the open seas.

"We have a strong sense of tradition here in Wigfield. We're one of the only towns that still celebrates V-J Day. For you young 'uns, that stands for victory over the Japanese! It's a joyous celebration. It's a time when the town comes together and remembers how many gave away their lives to nobly advance the cause of liberty, but mostly it's a good way to get together to remember how much we hate the Japanese. We hate Koreans, too! Sometimes it gets confusing telling them apart, but a simple way to do it is to remember one makes a delicious pickled spicy cabbage, and the other massacred our boys at Iwo Jima. The celebration is a whole-day event. We have a parade, usually one of the mayors makes a speech, then we stage the dropping of the bomb on Nagasaki. The kids make a mushroom cloud out of crepe paper and flour paste. In the evening, after the beer garden closes, someone from town dresses up like Tojo and we chase him down the street with sticks and bottles. Lord help him if we catch him! This one year, we got our hands on one of the Tojos over by where the school burned down and, oh my land . . . oh wait a minute, that wasn't during V-J Day, that was Martin Luther King Day, and it was the guy playing Jesse Jackson. The point is, this town knows how to celebrate!

"So much tradition will be lost if they tear down the damn dam! Where else are you going to go where all the folks are banded together? There is no color line here. None of that segregation. Everyone's the same here, as long as everyone's the same. And if they're not, well, things can get pretty ugly pretty quick. I remember once, one of the Hutsell twins, the one that got most of the spine after they were separated, brought home a new fella from the city who was uh . . . well, let's just say he knew the value of a diamond when he saw it. Anyway, the two of them were hanging out playing foosball, drinkin' and whooping it up over at the library. Well, some words were exchanged. Apparently Lars, Lars Koger, who was bartending at the library that night, and who is not too keen on strangers anyway, took a dislike to this hook-nosed fella. Lars has been a bit on edge since he lost his family to that series of shotgun accidents. Anyway, things heated up a bit, so Lars took a few playful 'stabs' at the young stranger with a carving knife. The rest of the boys in the bar tried to break up the scuffle by ending it quickly in favor of Lars. After all was said and done, that new fella looked like a blind man's jack-o'-lantern. But that is the thing about Wigfield—unity! People don't understand that about a small town. It's not like the big city, where a bunch of strangers are wandering around. I don't know what I would do if we were all forced to move. In a big city, someone my age would be vulnerable. You become prey to the throngs of strangers who sniff at your well-worn haunches like ravenous coyotes. That's the beauty of a small town like Wigfield. Wigfield has few enough people so you know who to be afraid of, and it's a long list. I'm on it."

CHAPTER NINE

THE day had taken its toll. So many holes left in my story to fill. So little Spackle. And time was running out for these desperate people. The grim reaper stood above with his scythe raised high, ready to sweep all these lives into the pit of oblivion. But what about me? Don't I have needs? As the old saying goes, "All work and no play gets your book done on time." I decided to knock off for an unspecified amount of time and just unwind.

First I planned to immerse myself in the local offerings. Immediately my roving eye was caught by a flickering sign: THE BUNNY HUTCH. Yes, I thought. Some mindless entertainment. What I needed was a mental hammock for my aching brain. Art to soothe the soul. And what could be more relaxing than the rhythmic bouncing of an artist's breasts?

Much to my shock and dismay, this cultural enclave turned out to be a cultural enclave. The naked nubile jigglers turned out to be one guy in clam diggers and a kimono.

As I tried to leave, he cornered me in his theater-in-the-round. I attempted to explain my mistake, but he would have none of it. He coaxed me into one of the few folding chairs facing the tiny stage. As the unmistakable acrid whiff of rodent urine bore down on me, he brushed aside a cluster of pellets, sat on the edge of the stage, and talked at me, stopping only to punctuate his points with long dramatic pauses.

JULIAN CHILDS

"I believe that the Arts define a community. And in this community I am the Arts. So in a way I am Wigfield. Especially with this dam tearing down business looming over us. More than ever the theater is the lifeblood of a community, but it's more than that. It's all the fluids, blood, semen, urine, *and* saliva. If I don't leave that combination of liquids in a puddle onstage after a performance, then I know I have dropped the ball and let my audience down. I for one am not going to let anything stop the theater. I have faced harder challenges. It's not the first time this theater has been threatened. I walk a tightrope on the edge of extinction every day! Yes, I have had to engage in some pretty unsavory activities to keep this little dream factory afloat. But I did, and no one can prove it, and that is all I am going to say about that without my lawyer present. I'll tell you one thing: I am not going to let them win. I am going to scream, yell, and stamp my little hoofies until someone pays attention to me.

"We have a great season planned for this year. And you'll notice that I used the term *year*. This is not going away in a month. You can't kill the theater. It's immortal. It's not like some human body that you could meet at a bar, pretend to be interested in, and then lure back to your theater so you can spike its drink with phenobarbitals and then

do unspeakable things to him. Just because you're an Artist doesn't mean you don't find that lifestyle offensive! And there has to be some retribution for those who would assume otherwise.

"This season we are doing *Velveteen Rabbit*—with real rabbits! Quite a treat for kids and adults alike. Following this, we are presenting *Children of a Lesser God*, also with real rabbits. Not every play will lend itself to real rabbits, but almost every play. When I founded this theater I was a little frustrated that no one in town seemed all that interested in joining the repertory company. I did get some interest from one of the dancers to take the lead in the *Nutcracker,* but her legs went bad on me. Those barrel dances really take a toll on the ladies. Not that I'm unhappy with my floppy-eared ensemble. They are industrious, they are dedicated, and they are delicious! I was thinking about commemorating the town's year-and-a-half centennial with a performance about the dam. I thought it would be entertaining as well as informative to make a working model of the dam and dress up my bunnies as various people in the town and then drown them. I really think it would make a statement about how I feel about certain people in town. Not that I'm bitter. I have a sense of humor about myself. How could I not? I mean with a town full of such cut-ups like Lenare.

"I love this town. The proof of that is that I still live here. I mean, if I didn't why haven't I left? I know there must be better opportunities out there. Based on just my enthusiasm alone, I'm sure I could work in any of the big theater cities—New York, Chicago, Jessup. Any of the biggies. But yet I remain here in Wigfield. Why? I must love this place. What alternative reason can there be? I mean, I can think of a few, but they are all just too depressing to be true. So I accept that I love it here in Wigfield and let's just leave it at that."

TEN

CHAPTER TEN

I'LL be the first to admit that literarily, I literally was losing hope of delivering this book on time, unless my publishers were suddenly willing to accept some factor of 50,000 that wasn't 50,000. There is no question that words had become a hot commodity, each like a diamond stolen from its cozy home inside an oyster. But I couldn't bear to listen to another anecdote. My brain had shut down and the only way to revitalize it was to get some serious R & R, and by R & R I meant, of course, T & A.

I soon found myself in front of the Twat Stop. Certainly an intriguing name, but I had already been fooled once. I decided to pop my head in for a cautious peek. As I cracked the door, I was immediately hit in the face with the smell of stale beer and human fluid. Welcome home. I strolled in and reclined on a seat next to the stage. Over the next few dances I became intimately acquainted with Raven, a big-boned temptress who was as impressed with my credentials as I was with hers. We decided to exchange professional courtesies in the dressing room. Never was I so anxious to get through an interview.

RAVEN

✤

"It's funny what ends up being home. Take me and Wigfield. I never planned to live here. I have to admit, if I was driving I wouldn't have stopped here. But as luck would have it, I wasn't driving, I was riding, handcuffed in the back of a police car. Now I work at the Twat Stop, which is the most sophisticated club in town.

"When I first heard about the dam being torn down I was on a three-day X freak-out, so I was mostly just amused. Three days later I was pretty tired and after that I was unconscious, but now I'm just taking it one day at a time, you know, just trying to figure out what I was saying. What was the question?

"The dam, right, the dam. I can say this about the dam. My friend Gwen and I were headed out to the woods because we heard that Spider was tappin' a half-barrel up on the trestle. When we got there it was more like a pony keg first of all, and second, Gwen's ex-boyfriend Mickey was there and he laid into her. And she's like, who do you think you are? You don't own me motherfucker, so he cuts her, and she's wearing my rabbit coat that I just got from that new girl CJ. I traded a pair of boots for it, after she set my couch on fire. They had these rockin' five-inch heels but they were too small. You got to have at least a five-inch heel. The regulars like the high heel cuz it adds length to your ass. It gives you a lengthy ass. I learned that when I was working at the Muff-iteria. The girls there all had these high-heeled boots and I was wearing a moccasin. They went with my character. Anyway, I once hit this windshield so hard with my head that it left a clump of hair in the crack. That's how they found out it was me. They traced the clump back to my scalp. But because the chick never regained consciousness, I got off. So now everything is cool except when every once in a while my scalp flares up and I have

to put a bag of frozen peas on the lump. Anyway, I guess that's what I think about the dam and whatever.

"I could easily describe Wigfield in three words, but I don't know what they would be. I think one of the best things about Wigfield for me is that I can walk to work. It's a real convenience. If the speakers are really cranked up at the club I can still be in bed when I hear Arby intro me over the PA system and all I have to do is roll off the mattress, shit, shower, and shave, and I can be on the runway so fast that the pole is still warm. And if there is one thing I've learned, it's if you don't put it out there, they won't put it in there. Sure, walking to work means I'm walking home from work, and yes that makes me easier to follow, but I'm sure that's a common problem with any job that involves truckers and alcohol. The government thinks they can just flood this town and nobody is going to say nothing. Well, they're wrong. I spend a lot of time thinking of things to say."

CHAPTER ELEVEN

FEELING spent from my repeated consultations with Raven, I wander back toward the Grimmetts'. A perfect night for a stroll. It is a lovely evening. A typical Wigfield evening. I notice the gentle steam rising from the random piles of earth, as if the mounds of slag were actually giant black apple pies just pulled from the oven. The sky glows red and swirls of gray clouds dance like newspaper blowing in an alley. The night is illuminated by the various fires burning in the distance like dozens of eternal flames honoring this picturesque village. Of course, the cruel irony is that these eternal flames are in constant danger of being extinguished forever by a river unleashed.

As I continue my journey I soak up the quiet. It was quiet. Quiet in that unique small-town way. In the big city the sound never stops, it's a blur of noise blending together into a cacophony of unidentifiable racket. But here, silence dominates. It's a silence one has to hear. This is the kind of quiet that almost acts as a band shell for the random sounds of the night. Allowing them to stand out in the spotlight for their solo performance. There is no mistaking the chirp of the crickets, or the roar of the semis or the nearness of those gunshots . . . I decide to pick up my pace.

By the time I reach the Grimmetts', I'm at a full sprint. It seemed like a fine night for a panicked dash. It's good to be home. After piling some furniture in front of the door, I stroll around the empty house. The Grimmetts have gone off to bed, probably hours ago. I myself am feeling a little wired, due either to the anxiety about finishing the book or that bottle of cough medicine I split with Raven. As the old saying goes, "An ounce of prevention is worth a pound of cure." It is essential I stay healthy until this book is finished, and given the amount of syrup I ingested, I feel confident I will not be troubled with a cough for years. I wander around the Grimmetts' charming domicile, making laps around the table like a racewalker trying to get to the finish line before his pupils explode. I notice a few old books on a shelf and in order to break my circular pattern, I make my way over. A certain book catches my eye, *The History of Wigfield*. This appears to be a book I would be interested in paraphrasing. I pull the book from its place and blow the dust from the top. It has a dank, musty smell. The smell brings back some wonderful memories of when I was a boy staying at my grandmother's house. In order to expand my horizons and their cocktail hour, often my folks would drop me off at Grandma's for my teen years. One rainy summer afternoon when Grandma was out—on the couch—I decided to search for something to end the boredom. Noticing a cord hanging from the ceiling, I wrapped it firmly around my neck and jumped from the stool. Much to my disappointed delight, the cord was attached to a staircase hidden in the ceiling. I ascended the secret steps into a dark cobweb-filled room packed with boxes, old furniture, and boxes of old furniture. I stumbled upon a collection of intriguing old books. I had never read a book and I was excited about my discovery. I dragged the heavy box over the attic rafters to a lone window so I could get a better look. I glanced out the window down into the yard. I had never been in my grandma's attic and I was impressed by how high up it was. I opened the window and looked below to see my grandmother had somehow made her way to the porch, where she lay passed out next to the hammock. A frightening thought suddenly crossed my mind: What would happen if one of these books accidentally fell from the attic window, or even more unthinkable, a series of them? I was appalled at my grandma's irresponsibility. What was she thinking, having all these heavy, loose books in an attic directly above where her skull was asleep? The horrifying scenario began to play out just as I feared. A book, almost as if under its own power, and lifted by me, made its way to the ledge. It began to teeter, and then just as inexplicably, totter. I attempted to scream out, to warn my grandmother asleep below, but my lungs were frozen by the fear that the sudden noise would wake her. The book began to rock back and forth more urgently now, clearly determined to strike its drop zone. Had only I known what kind of danger lurked in my grandmother's attic, I could have helped her somehow avoid this disaster. And then, like a six-pound pinecone being thrown by a tree, the book hurtled skullward.

As we grow older, we find that certain sense memories never leave us. Whether we like it or not, many of these experiences remain branded upon our gray matter for life. For example, the dull, dense sound an unabridged dictionary makes when connecting with the brain bone of a sleeping old woman is not one of the easier recollections to shake. I guess the point of my story is I love books. It's reading I hate.

As I held *The History of Wigfield* in my hands, fiddling with its well-worn cover, I anticipated the wealth of information it must contain. I excitedly cracked open the cover and the words seemed to leap right off the page and land directly in my book in identical sequence!

THE ORIGIN OF THE NAME WIGFIELD

(Liberally excerpted from *The History of Wigfield*)

The town of Wigfield takes its name from Civil War hero Captain Beauregard "Puddingfoot" Wigfield, a light cavalry officer who was so renowned for his cunning and speed in moving his troops that he alone among com-

manders miraculously avoided combat for the entirety of the Civil War. He is generally credited with instituting a radical guerrilla-type warfare in which he would quickly hide his entire regiment behind a small cluster of trees in response to an approaching army and stay concealed for days. He had the ability to camouflage the unit so ingeniously that they could remain undiscovered even though a crucial battle was raging only a few yards away. Stonewall Jackson once said of Wigfield, "Ol' Puddingfoot has everything you could want in a field commander: tenacity, celerity, and ingenuity! If only we could get him near a battlefield!" Arriving an hour and a half late for Pickett's charge, he took one look at the smoking field, covered with 3,000 dead or dying Confederate soldiers, held up a paper and famously shouted to his men, "Who wrote these directions?!"

As a field officer, he amassed an impressive record. He almost fought at the battle of Vicksburg. He was nearly a factor at Second Manassas. Lee went to his grave convinced that Wigfield would have turned the tide at Antietam if only he had participated. Renowned for his independent spirit, Wigfield refused to take orders to go into battles without a lengthy analysis and repeated confirmations of the order. He so feared Northern spies that he regarded every call to battle as a possible trap being laid by General Grant. He was so careful in this regard, so cautious of a ruse, that on the rare occasions he found himself near a battle, he would observe from a great distance through a spyglass, determined to make sure that the soldiers dressed in gray being viciously slaughtered were actual Confederate troops and not simply a Northern decoy.

Like many of the men torn from their homes during the War Between the States, Wigfield found solace in his infrequent letters home.

My dearest Martha,

The frosted fields of Virginia now act as a tomb to the thousands of Confederate troops who lie stiff on the field of Honor, their blood spilled in pursuit of fading victory like seeds onto barren ground. These young men once held the Cause so close to their bosoms only to have it ripped away by the War of Northern Aggression. In response to this Yankee onslaught, I am following a hunch and have marched my men to Miami in hopes of cutting off Sherman's supply of sugarcane and tangerines. Myself, as well as my men and me, are forced to seek refuge from the heat of the Florida sun at one of its many beachheads. You mustn't worry, Martha. Although we know war is an unpredictable beast, I will do my utmost to return to you and your family's beautiful and highly profitable plantation.

I think of you always, if not occasionally,

Love, Beau.

After spending months assuring himself that no citrus products were leaking from Florida above the Mason-Dixon line, Captain Wigfield marched his entire regiment to the defense of Richmond by way of the Oregon Trail.

But Fate would have her fickle way with this crafty ol' 'possum. Following a feast celebrating the fact that he found some food, Wigfield unexpectedly came upon a seemingly ragtag regiment of poorly armed Northern irregular troops, who approached with a white flag, hoping for a meal. But Wigfield was not so easily outfoxed. In an apparent attempt to simultaneously flank his Northern opponents and then lull them into a false sense of security, the entire regiment led by Wigfield quickly abandoned their posts, dropped their weapons, and retreated toward the Fresh Springs River, where disaster lurked. In the chaotic rush to encircle the Northern army by running away, Wigfield's entire regiment drowned in the rushing current of the river. The Northern commander recalled in later years, "I have to admit, I was completely fooled. I had no idea they were planning to flank us. After they dropped their weapons and ran screaming like frightened children I was convinced they were scared of us. As my men and I watched from the banks it never occurred to me how lucky we were. Had they not trampled each other in that river, who knows what kind of hell I would have marched my troops into." Wigfield was posthumously decorated by Confederate president Jefferson Davis, who said during the ceremony, "I didn't know the man personally, I never met him. Nor have I been made aware of any of his exploits that would be deserving of this or any medal." Words that, over a century and a half later, are still showing up in books like this.

TWELVE

CHAPTER TWELVE

IT seems that the major result of consuming what the less medically inclined might describe as a hazardous amount of cough syrup is a ravenous appetite. My attempts to roust Mrs. Grimmett from her sleep chamber in the hopes she would fire up the skillet proved that there was a limit to small-town hospitality. I decided to seek the fatted calf elsewhere. My journey quickly ended at the only eating establishment open at four-thirty A.M. It was a quaint little hamburger joint surrounded by a dozen or so idling semis, their great diesel lungs belting out a deep jazz riff through the horns of their smokestacks, exhaust caps flapping rhythmically like trumpet mutes. If one were so bold as to indulge in another truck metaphor, they could also be compared to a pack of dogs waiting patiently for their masters, their eighteen great rubber paws gripping the pavement, panting gouts of black diesel breath into the night sky. I'm sure other metaphors are out there as well. For instance, the trucks are wagons around an encampment, waiting for the Indians to attack from the strip clubs. I guess the exhaust would be smoke signals. Maybe one of the pioneers knows how to make smoke signals, and he's asking for a truce, or maybe there's a double agent. Hey, here's another one! The trucks are whales, the smoke is the waterspout and the truckers . . . are Jonah . . . coming back from a strip club.

At the center of this circle of metal giants was the aforementioned restaurant, Mack Donald's.

Slouching behind the counter was a sullen youth whose face bore the proud pox of deep midadolescence. He was engrossed in a pencil sketch he was rendering on the wall above the deep-fat fryer. As I approached the counter, I saw that it was one of a series of drawings on the wall, each depicting some large, demonic creature being devoured alive by some larger, demonic-er creature.

I enjoy being ignored by service personnel as much as the next customer, but I eventually cleared my throat to get the budding muralist's attention. Nothing. So, upping the ante a hair, I tossed a handful of ketchup packets into the fryer. This garnered both his attention and a stream of praise and profanity for my bold disregard of his safety. I placed my order while he toweled off the hot fat.

As my meal sizzled, we struck up an off-the-record conversation that I thoughtfully recorded.

DILLARD RANKIN

"I'm the night assistant manager here at Mack Donald's. I can't really spend that much time talking, 'cause I gotta keep my eye on the fry station. I got an order of onion rings, a cheeseburger, and a Cajun taco

salad in the basket. Fact is, that fryer is really the heart of the whole operation here. If that goes, there's no way for me to cook anything. It's a lucky thing about food. Everything fries at the same rate. But you gotta pull it when it's golden brown. Especially the salad. 'Cause if there's one thing I've learned, it's you can't un-fry things. There's a point at which you have to let them go.

"But whatever, who cares, this job is just temporary. I'm only doing this until my band takes off.

"What do I think about the dam coming down? That's a complex issue for me at this point in time. As a nihilist, I should really just be thinking about myself, but the dam is hard to ignore. Its looming mass of nothingness is a metaphor for our godless universe. Upon the occasional I have left my mark upon it because, as I'm sure you can tell by my body adornment, I am an Artist of Doom. Cast your gaze into my bicep if you dare, there you will find a tattoo of chaos and destruction. Go ahead if you wish to stare into the lair of oblivion. But beware: Once ensnared, there is no escape from my upper arm. Look at it, it will transfix you. Behold the mouth of madness. Don't stare too long. I don't think of it as a tattoo, it's more of a talisman of evil. It's a hexagram. It's a demon trap. It protects me from the forces of darkness and turns them to thine own will. For your own safety, let me walk you through it. That's the evil eye, or Belial's eye, depends on who you ask. To the left of that is my humble tribute to my favorite Corpse-Metal super group Autopsy Turvy. It was supposed to be a flayed cadaver inverted, but, uh, it didn't really gel. Right above that you see the Demon Goat Dog, which represents depravity and rebellion and my love of dogs. This little fella here is modeled after my little fox terrier Skipper, who I rechristened Be'elz-cifer the Damned. He was my demon beast who guarded the gates of my private Hell. But he got hip dysplasia and we had to put him down. I don't want to talk about it.

"These are all my original designs. I'm going to put them on T-shirts. Take a look at my sketch pad. This first one here is the Baphomet, which is, of course, the inverted pentagram with the goat skull inside. I've got the Baphomet with wings, I thought the wings was a nice touch. Makes it look like the Baphomet is flying. Can you imagine anything more evil? I can't. I got a claw holding a cross of bones, flaming cross of bones . . . burning cross of bones . . . inverted cross of bones . . . and a flaming inverted cross of bones with wings inside a Baphomet. Here's something I'm working on, it's a bloody inverted pentagram made of bone crosses with a screaming skull inside, and if you look closely, you can see inside the screaming skull's mouth—a little Baphomet. As soon as I save up some cash, me and the band are going on tour, and we'll sell my T-shirts. I just need a band and a way to get artwork on T-shirts. Oh, shit. The salad's burning. Great. . . . well, I'll just drown it in dressing.

"Anyway, like I was saying, pretty soon I'll be hitting the road with my girlfriend Regina. I guess we're getting married. It's sort of a preemptive strike. Everybody figures it's inevitable that she's gonna get knocked up, there's just no way to prevent it, so I guess this is like a shotgun wedding, just no bullets in the gun.

"The band is going to be just like Autopsy Turvy. I'm thinking of calling it Kill-icide. I've even got these lyrics that I wrote. Don't pay any attention that they're written down on this pink stationery in someone else's handwriting, and are inside this envelope addressed to me and sent by someone else and all. I guess I was trying to be ironic or detached or something, the point is, I wrote them. You're a writer, let me read 'em to you:

"Oh, Dillard . . ."

"Uh . . . I'm talking as somebody else here to myself, that's pretty creepy, huh? Anyway.

> "Oh, Dillard, without you I am in a cave,
>
> a cave of despair,
>
> a pocket of air trapped in a mountain of grief.
>
> The avalanche of indifference that you have unleashed
>
> has blocked, has sealed the mouth of this chamber

and entombed me in a blackness of choking denial.

Like an Egyptian mummy by the Nile

Waiting for her archaeologist

To dump his girlfriend

And spread open her sarcophagus

Come raid my treasures.

Love, Carla"

"I'll probably cut that 'Love, Carla' stuff. I don't even get it. Now just imagine those words coming out of my mouth along with a lot of blood. All backed by the hardest-core thrash-speed Corpse-Metal mayhem you can imagine. Did I say I was gonna effect my voice to sound like I'm Satan? 'Cause I am.

"So you can see, I don't give a shit if the dam comes down. I'm out of here the first chance I get. Mr. Hollinger is gonna have to find somebody else to fry his meals. I'm gone like a trucker at dawn. Hey, that's pretty good . . . that could be part of my song. I'll just tack it on the end of that other stuff I . . . wrote.

"Are you staring at my mouth? This isn't a harelip, it's a birthmark. It's probably aggravated. I slept on it funny. Anyway, here's your onion rings, cheeseburger, and taco salad fried to your perfection. And you had the malt liquor shake. If you want, you can eat that here. My shift's over, but I'm gonna hang out till the sun comes up. I don't like being on the streets alone after dark. Creeps me out."

I accepted Dillard's kind offer, scooted into a red-vinyl booth and set fork to the steaming golden crust of my lettuce. Casting about for some form of entertainment, I happened upon the latest edition of the local daily newspaper, the *Wigfield Sporadic*.

There is nothing quite like the folksy charm of a small-town periodical, with its tales of village life and the troubles thereof. To convey what the paper as a whole is like, I have included here an excerpt of the whole paper.

𝔚𝔦𝔤𝔣𝔦𝔢𝔩𝔡 𝔖𝔭𝔬𝔯𝔞𝔡𝔦𝔠

BREAKS IN THE WIGFIELD MASSACRE INVESTIGATION

By ENNIS CHISOLM

WIGFIELD, Sept. 4—There have been three separate breaks in the Wigfield massacre investigation. Yesterday, Hoyt Gein, police chief under Mayor Charles Halstead, accused Mayors Fleet Hollinger and Burchal Sawyer of obstructing his investigation. Meanwhile, Mayor Fleet Hollinger unveiled a revised list of top suspects, most of whom are Hoyt Gein. Mayor Burchal Sawyer was also named. In addition, during an exclusive press conference, Mayor Sawyer in a shocking revelation revealed the following revelatory information: He didn't do it and Fleet Hollinger and Hoyt Gein probably did.

More—See Style Section.

Cat Found in Tree. Tree Felled.

(story p. 3)

MYSTERIOUS SEEPAGE RETURNS

By ENNIS CHISOLM

WIGFIELD, Sept. 4—Any persons or person with business north of the Tit Time Show Palace should avoid contact or contacts with the brown foam clinging to the playground. This liquid has not been identified.

North Side of Town Quarantined

If you know or knew the origin or origins of the mystery liquid (gas?) please contact Fleet Hollinger at his place of business. The mercury and arsenic runoff pits have been ruled out as the source of the puzzling fluid.

Warrant of the Week

Wayne Jason "John" Waynes

Waynes is wanted for burglarizing a murder investigation site. He has brown hair and a blue eye. Police say he is either hiding at his home or at his job at the Quick-Stop off the interstate. If you have any information as to his whereabouts, please apprehend and bring him to justice. He is considered armed and dangerous.

Yesterday's Weather

Sunshine obscured by clouds
Air temperature: 59 degrees
Ground temperature:
108 degrees

Plutonium count:
17 parts per million.
Children and pets are discouraged.

With a belly full of cheese and ideas, I was all fired up for a nap. So I headed home for a predawn raid on slumberland.

CHAPTER THIRTEEN

DREAMS are funny things. Some say they are windows to our subconscious, others a foreshadowing of the future. Still others say that those first people were right with that thing about the subconscious. Who knows? All I know is that soon after my head hit the pillow, I found myself floating down a long hall that was, I think, also the interior of an artery filling up with fatty deposits. At the end of the hallway was a room bathed with golden light. In its center was a pedestal and upon this pedestal was a smaller pedestal, but upon that pedestal was a book. A large book. Thick. Beautifully thick. Like, 50,000 words thick. I floated closer to discern the title of this weighty tome. And there, upon its handsome hand-tooled leather cover, was the word "Wigfield"! *Wigfield*! by Russell Hokes! It was my book! What are the odds? I turned off my jet pack and settled to the floor, grasping for the book. Trembling with anticipation, I threw open the pages to the middle of the book and read the first sentence I saw. "I found myself floating down a long hall . . ." Yes! I flipped the pages frantically to see how the book ended, but just as I started to make out the first few words they would slither away like a sidewinder going for a pioneer toddler. I couldn't read any of it! On page after page, the letters swam and danced before my eyes like extras in a Busby Berkeley production. It was all gobbledygook!

I searched frantically for someone, anyone who could translate it for me, but everywhere I looked were just mirrors in which my own hideous laughing face was reflected. I cried, "How will I ever finish this book?" And then I knew the terrifying answer. I would have to write it.

I sat bolt upright in bed, my body bathed in sweat. As the sun sank below the horizon, I felt a stabbing pain in my abdomen. I quickly shuffled to the bathroom. Clearly, last night's deep-fat indulgence had exacted a heavy toll.

Having successfully dropped my payload, it was time to go back to the base to reload the bomb bay. As I entered the kitchen, I saw the Grimmetts walking onto their front porch for a postdinner smoke. It occurred to me that, while I had stayed here, Udell and Eleanor Grimmett had been wonderful guests in their home. A feeling of gratitude swept over me at that moment. They were so generous. How could I repay them in a form other than money? I decided to help by cleaning up the kitchen after them. What a nice surprise for them, I thought. First I would clean off the dishes, starting with the pie plate, which had inadvertently been filled with pie and left to bake in the oven at 350 degrees. But before I could properly clean it of pie I had to cool it. Luckily I found a leftover gallon of ice cream sitting in the freezer. This quickly done, I cleaned up a few leftover dollars from their savings tin and like a magical sprite out of a fairy tale, hurriedly slipped out the back door so as to not interrupt their coming back into the kitchen.

I felt good. My tummy was full, I had a few dollars in my pocket, and I was back on the trail of Fleet Hollinger. Where was this golden goose, and why was he so protective of those eggs I needed to steal in order to finish my book? It seemed clear that Fleet Hollinger was the lightbulb that all the town moths were flitting around. I needed to get to him before my deadline flipped off the porch light. My search led me to the edge of the woods. Fleet's daughter, Carla, had informed me that her mother, Fleet's ex-wife, Dorothy, now known as Thea, was living just outside of town with her protégée, Judy Brown, now known as Amythys. I followed the heady scent of sandalwood and the deep musky tang of natural human toward the giant inverted cross, and there, lit by the moon, was the shadowy image of a woman, her arms draped in black and flapping like some great flightless bird, but not an ostrich. Lying upon what appeared to be a great stone monolith, but was revealed to be a discarded meat freezer topped in animal hide, was the unclad, birthday-suited, bare-bodied nubileness of a healthy young woman, her back arched, her firm breasts saluting the moon like an eager private in a werewolf army. What had I stumbled upon? My first instinct was to not interrupt this most private of interactions, so I respectfully hid behind a tree where I had a clear view and let nature take its unnatural course. It occurred to me that one could be a jour-nalist for years, spend a lifetime pavement-pounding, lead-following, and fact-checking, and never come across a story this worthy of journalizing. I had happened upon the story of a lifetime, and I intended to leave no stone unturned. As I attempted to focus with white-hot intensity on what was clearly the heart of the story, the meaty one clad in black stepped into my line of sight, raised two chalices filled with dark viscous fluids above her ample head and began to chant in an unintelligible yet bone-chilling tongue. She moved in, hovering over the naked good-looking one I could no longer see, the wind blowing her cape like the tent flap on a Bedouin's hovel. She then emp-tied the contents of the goblets onto the young and thinner one who began to moan rhythmically. As I watched from the cover of darkness, one thought immediately leapt to my brain, "You're blocking my view!" I was not going to let my story slip away at this point—I had come too far and was too emotionally invested. I decided to change vantage points, and this proved my undoing. Because of the current state of my trousers, my movement was suddenly reduced to a halting shuffle, my feet ensnared in a tangle of twigs and poly-cotton. By the time my lower half had communicated its predicament to my upper half, my head, which has always had a mind of its own, was at full sprint. Philosophers have long pondered the question, If a tree falls in the forest and no one is there to hear it, does it make a sound? Who cares? I think my nose is broken. This much is clear. The chubby one heard it all, because now she was marauding toward me carrying a sword, like a one-woman Mongol horde.

After quickly righting my pantaloons, I set myself upon my knees before the approaching Chunk-ernaut.

My head began to sweat like a hunk of unrefrigerated cheese. I thought to myself, "What do I have to worry about? It's not like I'm an interloper. I am a journalist!"

My plan was simple. Stay calm and stay in control of what was becoming an increasingly dangerous situation. In order to implement my plan, I launched into phase one: begging for my life. When it appeared to the giantess that I meant no harm, she became slightly less aggressive, but by no means had I defanged this portly tiger. With the tip of her sword stuck into the base of my sternum, I calmly explained through a hail of tears and spit that I was a jour-nalist. I assured her that I was only here to help her and the town of Wig-field. She seemed curious to know whether or not I had spoken with Fleet Hollinger, which I assured her I hadn't. After reassuring her that she could say anything about anybody and I would print it, she relaxed and pulled the point from my chest, leaving a mark that would function as a souvenir of this chance encounter. Before we spoke on record, I encouraged her to complete whatever it was she was doing, but before I could finish the sentence, the young beauty leapt from the altar, quickly robed, and scampered into the forest. I volunteered to go after her but was informed that the "lunar tides were no longer in conjunction," or whatever, and we should move on with the interview. To avoid the possibility of again raising her thickly tufted hackles, I agreed.

HIGH PRIESTESS THEA

"I'm a witch along with my life partner du jour, Amythys. Most people think witches are a coven of lesbians dancing naked in the forest celebrating the semen stolen from imprisoned hypnotized males, which they then use to inseminate one another using turkey basters in order to create a legion of demon babies. Well, that's only part of it. We are also active in community outreach programs. People in this town dislike us because they misunderstand us. But it's all laid out clearly in the words we chant over our victims . . .

"Bide the Wiccan law ye must
Ropes that bind and dagger thrust!
Ne'er turn your back and never trust
But ever dread our demon lust!

"What ye sent forth come back to thee
Fire and Fang and fear times three!
Torment awaits your treachery
While we scream with mirthless glee!

"And that's pretty much where we're coming from. It's sort of a celebration of nature. I don't understand the animosity that people feel toward us. I know some people have even blamed us for this

dam situation, like we've placed some sort of curse on the town or something. Sometimes this place is like Old Salem, hunting for witches because of ignorance. If only they'd reach out and try to understand what we're about, we wouldn't feel compelled to place curses on them. Anyway, we don't want the dam to be torn down. We never want to leave this place. Sure, in the big city you can be anonymous, but in a town like Wigfield you can rule the night.

"Before I talk about anything else, I'd first like to educate people to what we witches are about. All fear is based on ignorance. First of all, we are witches who practice wicca, which is different from a wiccan. A wiccan is a wicca who practices witchcraft. The philosophies behind a witch and a wiccan are totally different. A wiccan wears ceremonial black robes and invites her body to be inhabited by an evil spirit that commands her to perform tasks of mayhem and destruction. A witch, on the other hand, can wear anything she wants. And it's as simple as that. We don't ride around on broomsticks. We don't have cauldrons full of boiling witch's brew. We don't have green skin with warts on our noses and long stringy hair. We are just like everybody else provided everybody else is a witch, which I doubt because they don't show up to any of the meetings.

"Now let me tell you a little something about Fleet Hollinger. First, I'd like to comment on some of my previous rebuttals regarding some earlier statements I made in reference to rumors that have been spread by my former life partner Fleet Hollinger. Notice I say life partner and not husband, because the husband/wife relationship is a relic of the patriarchal power structure. I don't believe in the institution of marriage, unless there is some monetary settlement involved. I would like to rescind the retraction of my statement denying any involvement with the unsolved Wigfield murders known as the Wigfield Eight, previously known as the Wigfield Six. You see, I don't need to deny it because all I said was 'The only person I want dead is Fleet Hollinger, and I would be willing to build a staircase of human sacrifices to get to him!' Now, I don't know what set off the alarm bells, but I've got some pretty disturbing theories.

"Number one, religious bigotry. The fact is, if you have the courage to be a pantheistic pagan who believes in sowing the seeds of chaos in order to feed the belly of the Dark Father, you are going to raise a few eyebrows in a small backwater town. Sorry folks, we can't all be Presbyterians.

"Two, Fleet Hollinger. Fleet Hollinger would do anything or say anything in order to destroy me because he cannot stand the fact that I am liberated, I've found my perfect life mate, and I can bend reality using only a candle and some chicken blood.

"Three, I might of done it.

"Four, jealousy. The whole town is jealous of me because I make a very comfortable living at my roadside stand selling candles shaped in the glorious naked likeness of my life partner, Amythys. I also sell photos of my life partner celebrating her womanliness in many suggestive poses. Sometimes a businesswoman is intimidating to backward thinkers. Well, that's their problem, not mine. So, I am going to continue to live my life and Amythys's as I see fit. And nobody, especially not Fleet Hollinger, is going to change that."

After finishing my tête-à-tête with the high priestess, I consumed a form of tea that she referred to as Tiamat's milk. Three hours later, I was surprised to find that I had been unconscious. It was an unexpected nap, especially given the amount of sleep I had stored away over the past week. I did happen to find myself quite refreshed, as well as frightened and naked. I gathered my clothes from the ceremonial bone altar they had somehow found themselves ritually draped upon and took a lazy stroll in the form of a panicked run back toward town.

CHAPTER FOURTEEN

FEAR is a funny thing. If that's true, why aren't I laughing? I have a growing anxiety, which like a ravenous blue jay has been picking at my brain, as if my skull had been hollowed out, painted to resemble a miniature church, hung from a tree limb, and loaded with seed. Until now my tactic in combating this dread has been not to acknowledge it, to keep it locked up so tightly inside me that it can't get any air and will suffocate on my self-control. But keeping feelings bottled up is like holding an angry tiger by the tail: Unless you hold on tight, he'll kill you—metaphorically. Realistically, if you have a tiger by the tail, he'll kill you whether you hold on or not. In fact, if you hold his tail he'll probably find you quicker. All he has to do is follow his body down to the end of his tail, and there you are. But not for long. Sure, technically you might be able to continue holding on to the tail while he is gnawing on your skull, but this is merely muscle reflex. Let's face it, once the head leaves the body, you aren't doing much of anything. I guess my point is, don't touch tigers' tails. They don't like it. They are very flexible and have powerful paws with razor sharp, retractable claws. I don't even want to talk about the teeth.

I have decided to change my tactic. I will expose my fear. I will no longer attempt to wrestle it into submission. I will put it down for all to read. My guess is that once my fear is uncovered and left lying naked and bare for all to see, it will tremble in humiliation and then shrivel into obscurity. Well, here goes. My fear is:

There is no way in hell I will ever complete this book!

Nope. That didn't work. If anything, that just served to sharpen the edge of my terror. My God, it's burning. This isn't good at all . . . I've got to find some way to shove that fear back in me. It's fighting me . . . It's so strong . . . Jesus, it's huge. How did something that big come out of me? Get back in there! Damn you! Get! Back! In!

I realize at this point that there are only two ways to alleviate my fear. One would be simply to finish the book. The other would be to stay heavily medicated.

Dr. Raja Chuhas is located in the center of town. I sat in a comfortable vinyl bucket seat in his waiting room while he attended to a stripper with an emergency implant rupture. Next to me, in the driver's seat, another patient, an elderly woman, waited. It was unclear what was ailing her, but by the look of her grizzled . . . skin? . . . I'd say it was urgent. We got to chatting. I explained about the book I was writing and the people I had talked to in town. She was anxious to contribute. So I set my waiting-room seat on recline, adjusted my headrest, and pressed PLAY on my recorder.

DOTTIE FORE

"I am the oldest person in town. You might have heard that Mae Ella Padgett is the oldest person in town. She struts around town saying she's the oldest person in town, but it's not true. The only thing old about her is that lie. I'll deal with her. I find it sad that some people, namely Mae Ella Padgett, have such meaningless lives that they have to grasp on to some insignificant title in order to feel like their life is not completely worthless. Pathetic really. Oh, did I mention I've also had the most dental work in town? My gums are diseased. They are retreating away from my teeth like a rat from a flame. That's why when you burn a rat make sure you've got it cornered. I am well into my late forties, and let me tell you I've seen a lot of towns and cities, enough to know how special Wigfield is. Wigfield is small, but that's what gives it its charm. In our town we don't even use addresses, we just say, 'I'll meet you by where the bodies were found,' or 'Meet me by where the parts of the bodies were found,' or 'I'll see you by the mercury spill,' and everybody will know what you're talking about. It's nice that way. In the last few years, some of the younger folks put on airs, saying, 'Meet me across from the children's park,' instead of the 'abandoned well,' but I guess you have to go with the times.

"I'm not trying to say we don't have problems like everybody else. That's the way life is. I remember not far back, I got some dogs to take care of and some chickens to take care of and the dogs killed my chickens, so I got rid of the dogs and got some more chickens and wouldn't you know it? *I* killed the chickens. I guess I judged those dogs pretty harshly. Who can blame them? All that cluckin' and plus me knowin' how good they taste and all. I guess what I'm saying is that just because we're small doesn't mean we don't have our share of problems. And Wigfield is small. It's so small that we have to go to the post office for a haircut, and they always lose it. It's a town so quiet

that you can't help but hear the imaginary band in my head. They don't have what you would call a large repertoire, and they may not be what you city folk would call 'real,' but Lord they're loud. My dead son Jake plays the cymbals. He fell down the children's playground, and we couldn't get him out. He was all I had left, and this town took him from me. But I don't blame the town for what they all did to me. I don't hold grudges.

"It's a great town. People ask me why I don't leave. Well, the answer is simple: Jake won't let me! He insists that I make the people of this town pay. Sometimes he takes over my limbs, and he makes me do things. He's a mischievous boy. He wants me to feed people down the playground. He never seems to get full. My home is here. The well is here. Once a week the lone bus stops in town, and if a straggler or two wanders off, the band in my head will strike up a boisterous march, and I know it's feeding time. My son must be fed.

"Twenty-three years ago I showed up in Wigfield carrying my infant son Jake, following the lead of Jake's father. He had arrived seven months ahead of us, and he had set up quite a nice little home for us in the trailer he was hiding in with that other woman. I had not planned to come to Wigfield, but now it's home. Now I have a house here, and I don't want to lose it. Everything I earned from welfare over the last twenty years I put into that house, and I'm pretty sure that Jake is not going to let me let anyone try to take it away."

Finally it was my turn to see the doctor. I squeezed between the waiting-room chairs into the office. Immediately I was impressed with the amount of shag carpeting. How did they get it to stick on the ceiling like that? The doctor himself was a richly tanned, be-bearded gentleman of indeterminate height. He looked up from his deep crouch and beamed at me. I settled onto my haunches and told him what I wanted. He understood immediately. He didn't put me through the usual physical. He didn't try my patience by having me fill out a stack of forms with meaningless questions like Are you allergic to any medications? He didn't waste my time writing out prescriptions. I merely placed an unmarked envelope with some cash on the table, and he slipped me some pills. Simple as that. After quickly ingesting a fistful of medication, I asked him to tell me his story.

DR. RAJA CHUHAS

"I love Wigfield. It reminds me of the quaint little town in Pakistan, called Gujarat, where I spent much of my early career. Like Wigfield, they understood the value of human life. So very few people are willing to put a price on it. Pakistan is where I learned the plastic surgeon trade. I cut my teeth in Gujarat by reshaping children's skulls so they would make more compelling beggars. Visitors always seem enamored with the small-headed ones. Life was good there, but eventually I became disillusioned with Pakistan after the government callously stamped out the begging syndicate. What happened to respect for tradition? When I came to Wigfield I could not believe my good fortune. Like Gujarat, many of the people in Wigfield understand that in order to connect with the consumer, alterations are necessary. I have turned my talent for creating pinheads into a lucrative business increasing breast size. And now, for the second time in my life, the government wants to intervene and destroy my livelihood! Why can't they leave me alone?

"I have made friends with many of the ladies who visit my plastic surgery van, and it's sad to think that if this dam comes down they

will no longer have a place to shake the incredibly large appendages I have worked so hard at creating. I don't want you to think that the only connection I have with these ladies is the silicone-filled bags I forced into their chests. I also remove fat from their hips, smooth out wrinkles, and for many of the girls attempt to cover old knife wounds.

"In much the same way a normal homeless child doesn't evoke sympathy, some of the older ladies who don't look so fresh don't get a positive reaction from the customers. But my policy is never to turn a customer away. Some doctors might tell their client, 'What you're asking me to do might be dangerous to you health,' or 'If this leaks inside your breast it's going to cause some major problems,' but I don't say those things. I'm not here to judge. I'm here to help. But the government wants to stop me from helping. Some people have said, 'Dr. Raja, if the dam comes down, why don't you go somewhere else to ply your trade, since your entire office is located inside a van?' Well, to these people I say, I can't imagine going anywhere else! Look, I'm a doctor, we all know that, but the people in Wigfield don't care about college and boards and exams and licenses. These things mean nothing to these people. They are interested in a friendly medicine man who is willing to do the things they ask without asking a lot of questions. It's a mutual respect. I don't ask them questions, and they don't ask me things like 'What college did you go to?' or 'Why don't you display your license on the side of the van?' or 'Are these tools clean?' Maybe I'm crazy, or maybe I think small, but I have to believe I would be hard-pressed to find another town with such an abundance of strippers who ask so few questions."

Following my discussion with Dr. Chuhas, I decided to temporarily suspend my hunt for Fleet Hollinger, at least until the pills wear off, cuz I don't care 'bout nothin', baby. I'm free. I flow wherever the wind takes me, and anywhere it takes me is groovy. I'm not trusting anyone over thirty, and I'm almost forty. Far out. Who cares about finishing books? Let them come and try to take back their advance, what are they gonna do, sue me? How can they sue me? I don't have a lawyer. I wonder what a lawyer costs? Am I going to have to hire a lawyer?! I don't have any money. I spent it all trying to write this stupid book. Damn, those pills wear off quickly.

CHAPTER FIFTEEN

DESPERATE to avoid a lawsuit, I decided to look up the man who probably knew more about this town than anybody else was willing to admit. Ennis Chisolm. He publishes the only newspaper in town. He's the editor in chief, the printer, the reporter, and the delivery boy. I found his can-do spirit inspirational. Of course, he's not writing a book like me, he's only writing a newspaper. A newspaper is a much simpler undertaking than what I'm attempting to pull off. A newspaper is merely a collection of stories and interviews with some photos.

As I sat down in Mr. Chisolm's office, the first thing I noticed about him was his wonderful sense of humor. I just had to laugh. His desk was littered with various joke items, one more hilarious then the next. He had a plastic dome filled with water. Floating in the water was a tiny hat, a pipe, a carrot, and some pieces of coal. The caption on the dome read, "Florida Snowman." Bull's-eye! What brilliant satire. It's about time somebody gave those Floridians a taste of their own mischief. There was also what appeared to be a can of soda that was on its side and had spilled out onto the desk. On closer inspection, the soda was dry and solid! What a scathing comment on the giant cola conglomerates. Kaboom! Take that, Tab!

As Chisolm reached across the desk to shake my hand, I knew I was going to hit it off with him, because there at the end of his arm was what had to be the classic joke rubber hand. I played along grasping his cold imitation man-paw as if it were actually flesh and bone, and then in order to turn the comic tables and keep us on equal footing, I decided to pluck off the humorous appendage. With a quick violent yank, I dragged him across the desk and onto the floor. The hand did not come free. Moaning in a confused daze, he demanded an explanation. I thought to myself, "This mischievous prankster really knows how to follow through with a joke!" Barely keeping a straight face, I kept up my end of the act, helping him to his feet and apologizing profusely for my clumsiness. He warily accepted and we got down to the journalistic business of interviewing.

ENNIS CHISOLM

"I'm the editor of the *Wigfield Sporadic*. The paper is a free daily that comes out whenever and costs a dollar. What do I think about the dam coming down? I love it, and I hate it! Let me explain. Love is a positive feeling of attraction and affection. Hate on the other hand is much more negative, it's a disdain, a repulsion. Let me explain further. I love the dam coming down because I'm a newsman, and this is the biggest story I'll ever cover, and it's happening right in my own backyard! Up till now, the biggest story I've covered would probably be the unsolved murder cases. But that became kind of tedious to report on when bodies kept piling up but no suspects did. I guess I've got my pet theories about who did it, but in each one, the finger always points back

to me, so I tend to keep them to myself. Maybe I committed the murders so I'd have something to write about. See what I mean? I guess it's better to not say anything. Anyway, that's why I love the dam coming down. Now, I hate the dam coming down because my one good story will soon be gone, and the very newspaper where I would write about it could soon be washed away. I have a hunch that this is ironic.

"I have to admit, until the dam story broke, I was thinking about cashing the paper in. Things were getting pretty bad. I would print the papers and set them outside the office, and the stack would just sit there. I gotta tell you, it's a little disheartening when you spend forty-five minutes writing and printing a paper, and then nobody reads it. It got to the point where I would just bring the whole stack back in and use them for my next edition. The paper was getting pretty hard to read, because I'd just print over the old articles. I would use different colored inks so the new edition would sort of stand out from the old one. Eventually it would look like a box of crayons on a radiator, but harder to read. With this dam coming down though, I'm starting to move papers again.

"I was pretty excited when I heard about this book being written. Finally, a fellow journalist to compare notes with. I love words. Next to vomit and maybe teeth, they are the most frequent things to come out of my mouth. When I heard another writer was in town, I had these fantasies about us having a two-man think tank. We would lock ourselves in a room and exchange ideas and barbs just like the Algonquin Round Table. I'd be like Alexander Wolcott, and he would be Dorothy Parker. He would sting me with his scathingly droll observations. He'd walk about the room shaking those hips in my face all the while cutting me to ribbons with that famous sarcastic wit. I'd be speechless, me, Alexander Wolcott speechless, not sure if it's because I've been bested in verbal sparring, or those eyes. Those deep black eyes and that cute little bob haircut. But then she goes too far, and in a sudden fury I rise from the table and grab her firmly around the shoulders and shout into her face, 'This time you've gone too far,

Dorothy Parker! This time you've gone too far!' And then I'd punctuate my argument with a long, deep, hard kiss. As I'd feel her bosom heave against my chest I'd think, 'What's the matter, Dorothy? Cat got your tongue?'

"Anyway, that's my story in black and white. I guess I'm sort of like the town crier. Except I shout with my ink instead of my lungs. Not that I'm a stranger to screaming. We have a hollering contest in town every year, and I always enter. You should stick around for it this year. The whole town turns out. We go up by the dam, because the echo is good. We make a whole day of it. People bring coolers. Fleet supplies some of his famous One-Fourth Pounders with Cheese. Mae Ella makes sausage cookies, and Dottie brings her beef potato salad. After we eat and drink our fill, it's time for the hollerin' contest. All the contestants line up. We check each other out to see who signed up that year. Some years the competition is pretty stiff. Everybody has their different techniques and their personal style. Then Fleet fires off a gun and it's time to start the contest. First we chase down the drifter and secure him, then we take turns doing things to him that make him holler. And the one that makes him holler the loudest wins. I've never won, but I've given it a run a few times. Most years Lenare Degroat takes top honors, and frankly, at this point, I'd be afraid to beat him, considering what he's done to some of those drifters. It's a lot of fun, but like most holidays, it's really for the kids.

"So, I guess what I'm saying is there is a lot of responsibility being the one whose job it is to get the word out. I've got to say I'm glad you're here writing this book. Now we're like a team informing the masses about the plight of Wigfield. Hey, we should get a name for the two of us. Something that really captures our personalities. You know like Newspaper Man and Book Boy or Print Man and his faithful sidekick Sidekick Boy. Or how about Dr. Chisolmstein and Igor? Hey, I got it, the Jolly Green Ennis and the Little Green Sprout. We're on a roll. We're jamming.

"Jeez, with your help, soon the whole world will know about this Representative Bill Farber and how he holds the fate of a town in his hands. After that, we can take on other injustices. We could even get outfits. How do you look in tights?"

After a delightful late afternoon spent spending the early evening talking with Ennis Chisolm, he asked me if he could interview me for his local paper. I said no. I'm writing a book, and that must remain my focus. I can't allow myself to be sidetracked helping others fill up their pages with words while my pages lie naked and shivering in the cool night air, calling out to me, "Cloak us in the warmth of your words!" But then I rethought the offer, and I said, "Absolutely not." I'm here in this town as an observer, not a participant! I am committed to following the writer's creed, which I'm certain probably exists. To be fair, I decided to meditate briefly on his proposal. It then became clear to me . . . yes. Why the change of heart? No reason. I suppose I'm fickle that way. I can only say that it had nothing to do with the possibility of reprinting a lengthy interview in a book I'm struggling to finish, a suggestion that I find insulting. Then something disturbing occurred to me. If I were to include his interview in my book, would Mr. Chisolm, as a professional interviewer in his own right, be entitled to royalties from my publication?

Let's get something straight here and now. I want to be absolutely clear about this. I have no problem whatsoever sharing what will be, I'm sure, if there is indeed any sort of justice in this world, a king's ransom of royalties generated from this book. Nothing would make me happier than to give part of my hard-earned money away to people I barely know and who have made minor contributions which in no way affect the success of this book one way or another. That's a given. My concern is of a legal nature. Even though I have no experience with literary law, it would be my uninformed guess that there is a thick web of legal complications regarding collecting royalties. In good faith, could I really drag what I'm tempted to refer to as a friend into a quagmire of lawyers and contracts just so he could receive a hefty chunk of change for so little work? What would that say about me? So, in order to shelter him from attorney-generated red tape, I declined the interview, but given the fact I now have a lengthy intro to an interview I am unwilling to grant, I decided to interview myself.

ME: "I first would like to say that I'm honored to have the opportunity to sit down with a writer of our caliber."

ME: "Thank you."

ME: "How long have you been a writer?"

ME: "What time is it?"

ME: (laughter) "Who would you say are your literary influences?"

ME: "I'm sorry, you've lost me. What do you mean by that question?"

ME: "Your guess is as good as mine."

ME: (laughter)

ME: (applause)

ME: "What are your plans after the book is published?"

ME: "A series of long vacations, punctuated by a number of illicit affairs."

ME: "Has your editor been helpful in the process of writing this book?"

ME: "I'm glad you brought that up."

ME: "I was hesitant. I wasn't sure it was a topic you would want to get into right now."

ME: "I think now is as good a time as any. To answer your question, I respect my editor, I communicate well with my editor, but I don't fully understand where my editor is coming from. For instance, when my manuscript in progress returns from my editor, I find some of my words crossed out and replaced by other words that are not mine. Now, how am I supposed to react to that?"

ME: "Why don't you attempt to describe your feelings? A word perhaps."

ME: "Betrayed . . ."

ME: "Go on."

ME: "Powerless . . ."

ME: "Yes."

ME: "And—I don't know what to make of this—but a little turned on."

ME: "Would you like to explore that feeling?"

ME: "With pleasure. Sometimes I feel like my editor is a stern disciplinarian paddling my taut buttock until it's fiery red because of some grammatical faux pas I committed on her pristine blackboard. Her chalk-covered hand coming down upon my hindquarters like a bed slat. Again and again and again, until my nether haunch is as tender as a veal picatta. You could cut it with a fork."

ME: "Oh my."

ME: "You asked."

ME: "Guilty as charged. Perhaps we should change course."

ME: "All right."

ME: "Let's talk a little about you."

ME: "Let's, my life is an open book."

ME: "What happened in Ohio?"

ME: (silence)

ME: "What happened in Ohio?"

ME: "Look, I put that part of my life behind me a long time ago."

ME: "Why don't you want to talk about it?"

ME: "This interview is over!"

ME: "Is it? Why do you carry the receipt to a storage locker located in Canton?"

ME: (silence)

ME: "What's in that storage locker?"

ME: "Look, I was traveling through Ohio, I acquired something that needed to be stored, and that's all I want to say about it."

ME: "Who's Helen?"

ME: (silence)

ME: "Does the name The Frolic Room mean anything to you?"

ME: (silence)

ME: "Let me ask two related questions: What happened to the pinky on your left hand, and why are you afraid of longshoremen?"

ME: "That's it! This interview is definitely over! I'm not going to be ambushed by somebody who I happen to know has a few of his own skeletons in his closet, and they are wearing some pretty dirty laundry."

ME: "You're bluffing."

ME: "Am I?"

ME: "I don't believe you."

ME: "Really? Who's Helen?"

ME: "I don't know any Helen."

ME: "Really, well, maybe I'll give her a little jingle and see if she knows you."

ME: "You wouldn't dare!"

ME: "Try me. I'm a desperate man."

ME: "I guess this interview is over."

CHAPTER SIXTEEN

THE interview over, I was visibly shaken, and wandered the street of Wigfield in order to regain composure. It occurred to me that I had now spoken to almost everyone in town, including me, but still Fleet Hollinger remained elusive. No matter where I looked for him, he was always elsewhere. I confronted the possibility that I might never get my interview.

Men react to adversity in many ways. Often we don't find out who we truly are until we've been tested.

Sometimes a challenge can spark the greatest in a man. When an impossible dream hangs just beyond our grasp, that's when we dig down inside for that extra effort, that painful sacrifice that will extend our reach and find us clutching a star.

Or it can teach us the nobility of graceful defeat. Finding honor even when being bested, like the athlete who, though he has been humiliated on the field, can still walk off with his head hung high, because he realizes that there will be another day, another chance at glory.

Or you can quit, which is what I'm doing.

Dear Hyperion Books,

   By the time you get this letter, I will be long gone, hunkered down in a terrain that it would be extremely difficult for a lawyer to traverse.

   I'm sorry it has come to this. We had such high hopes for this book. Or at least you did, judging by the size of my advance. I, on the other hand, was completely aware of my abilities.

   It was fun while the money lasted, and I hope there are no hard feelings. Sometimes these things don't work out. Don't blame yourself.

   I hope this letter finds you well.

                    Warm regards,
        Master Russell Horatio Hokes, Esq.

I stumbled about town, clutching the scrap of cocktail napkin this letter was written on, looking in vain for a post office or a mailbox. As I pondered my predicament, a long dark sedan that looked pieced together from various late models, joined with a patchwork of welds and liberal slatherings of bondo, cut off my path.

From the bowels of the vehicle emerged twin no-nonsense behemoths in greasy overalls. I was gripped by fear and then by their hands. What did they want? I asked. They merely tightened their hold on my bicep bones and told me we were going for a ride. The back seat must have been full, because they piled me into the trunk and locked me in for my comfort and safety. Alone in the stifling darkness, I decided to play it cool and scream like a frightened child.

Certain everyday objects become so familiar that we forget they even exist. For instance, no one gives a second thought to tire irons until you get a flat or one bangs against your temple for a forty-minute trunk ride.

Eventually the car came to a halt, the lid popped, and I was extracted from the trunk like a tooth from a bite wound. Where was I? I must have been pretty scrambled, because it appeared I was only about twenty yards from where they picked me up. The sign in front of me said it all: FLEET'S FLEET OF USED CARS.

Fleet's men grasped me again by the arms, and I was led up some steps into a front office. There, sitting behind a large desk, was the eponymous Fleet Hollinger. This was the moment I had waited for: an audience with the last mayor. Jackpot!

He sat there framed by a halo of used auto parts, distant as a god of ancient days, and I, the supplicant, stood before him like Moses on Mount Sinai. The silence stretched like a desert for what seemed like forty years, and my faith faltered. Was I right? Was this interview my Promised Land of Golden Fatted Calves? Then he spoke and the bush began to burn.

FLEET HOLLINGER

"I'm a simple man in a simple town. That's the whole seed in a nutshell. Small towns are built on old-time values. Friendliness, openness, trust. That's what I'm about. Let's take for instance my relationship with . . . you. I don't know you, don't know anything about you, but I am opening up to you. There is a level of trust being established. I'm a trusting guy. Now, it would be heartbreaking if that trust were ever . . . betrayed. There is no question that I would be angry, that is pretty much a given. Sure, I would want to lash out swiftly and viciously. We could pretty much count on me wanting to

see you pay. I mean literally see, while you pay, physically and repeatedly, your screams begging to end this brutal payback falling on deaf ears. Well, not so much deaf as amused. Nobody would question that, and I hope you don't. But the fact is I'm just a small-town businessmayor, what can I do? I don't have a gang of mindless thugs at my disposal who I sedate with call girls and auto parts and can unleash at a moment's notice. I don't have 'em. But why do I need 'em? I'm sure you are who you say you are and that you will represent me in a way befitting the tragic consequences if you don't.

"So, moving on, like I said, I'm a businessman. I own and operate a few of the businesses here in town. Besides the used car lot, I also own Fleet's Used Auto Parts. Fleet's Used Auto Parts is the oldest business in Wigfield. Over the years other fly-by-night used auto yards have popped up and then disappeared. People do business with me because with me the customer comes first. Take that place Burchal Sawyer runs down the road, you're not going to get the kind of friendly attention you're gonna get at Fleet's, or for that matter, knowledgeable. To me, an automobile is like the buffalo was to the Indian. I use all the parts. I can't believe those Indians killed all those buffalos. Fleet's Used Auto Parts is one of the proud Wigfield institutions that will be destroyed if they tear the dam down.

"Another business I run is Mack Donald's. The only and the best fast-food chain in Wigfield. As we speak, a large hamburger chain is trying to shut me down. I can't really mention their name because currently I'm avoiding a subpoena. Apparently you get in trouble in this country if you name a restaurant after yourself. I never even heard of that other restaurant. All I know is my middle name is Donald, and my nickname is Mack because this guy I know drives a truck. It seemed natural to me that a clown would be the mascot. How can they have a lock on that? When you think of hamburgers, you think of cows, cows make you think of bullfights, and who distracts the bulls? Clowns! I named the clown after my nephew Ronald. I wouldn't be surprised if that unnamed hamburger chain is involved with this whole dam thing. I bet they would love to see the dam torn down and their competition washed away. Well, I'm not going to lose any sleep over it. The way I look at it, justice will prevail. I guess what bothers me most is the way they take the high road with their fancy lawyers and everything. I bet that hamburger chain doesn't even use real hamburger meat. Why would they? I don't. There are a lot of things that taste like hamburger that are in no way related to a cow.

"The best hamburger we sell is the Large Mack. It's two all patties, extraordinary sauce, lettuce, squeezable cheese, pickled onions, on a set of buns. When you order the smiley meal you also get fries and a Cahoke. We make our own cola beverage, so it's gotta be good.

"Some people ask me why don't I avoid all this legal malarkey and just call my hamburger stand Fleet's Burgers. Well, I did for a while. And then I didn't, OK? Business was fine, but I just decided to close down for renovations. Thought I'd try a new name, added a few golden half loops on the sign, and all of a sudden I'm in a lawsuit. Well, if you can find a correlation between the name change and my sudden increase in business, then you get a lawyer and get in line.

"In addition to my used auto parts empire and my one-link hamburger chain, I also operate a number of gentlemen's clubs and morgues. You see, as a businessman, it's my job to find a hole and then fill it. You see what I'm talking about? I sensed a need for entertainment, a hole if you will, so I shoved it full of women willing to take their clothes off for minimum wage.

"Along with being a respected businessman, I'm also the mayor. You might have heard there are some other mayors around town. Well, that's just a lot of bunk. Everyone in town knows I was leading in the polls when that suspicious fire broke out at the polling station over at the firehouse. That was a dark day for this community. Somewhere between two and forty people died. Nobody knows for sure because one of the morgues which was next door to the fire-house, went up as well, and as we all know, it's difficult to tell one charred skeleton from another. One way to tell, of course, would have been to check dental records, which is why for years I've been pushing the town to keep dental records. How many corpses have to go unidentified before we get with the program? Incidentally, that was the major plank of my campaign—forced dental photography. Anyway, back to the fire: As the inferno roared, the fireman did his best, but God knows how tough it is to extinguish a fire when all your equipment is ablaze.

"After the tragedy, everyone on the ballot claimed victory. But during trying times like these it's important for this town to rally around one mayor. I think it's important that two of the three mayors relinquish power so we have strong leadership. Two of the three mayors need to be unselfish enough to put this town first and step down. That is why I humbly offered to accept their resignations. I think this game of theirs has gone on long enough. Fighting over leadership in a time of crisis is madness. Just the other day, one of their police chiefs ran my police chief off the road, causing him to plow into the side of the arsenic runoff containment tank, and his body was burned beyond recognition. He was as crisp as a pork rind. I guess the only upside of this whole mess is that, like I said, I instituted forced dental X-rays for all my appointees. You see, with most of the burnt carcasses we pull from the tank, it's anybody's guess what the identity is. But because in this situation we were able to match the bite plate, we knew exactly which widow to call. At least we have that to feel good about. Anyway, I'm sure this mayoral mix-up will all wash out in the blood bath. Incidentally, I feel like it would be a good time to point out that my home is completely shingled in discarded asbestos brake pads. It can't burn. Just a little note to anyone who might have an itchy lighter finger.

"I'm also a family man. I have a son, Fleet Jr., who is at the military academy up in Shell Knob, hopefully getting some of the pussy kicked out of him. And I have a beautiful daughter by the name of Carla. She is just the apple pie of my eye à la mode. I can't believe how fast she is growing up. Soon it will be time for her to meet a fella and settle down. Now, if this hypothetical fella knows what's good for him, he'll treat her right. 'Cause I'm gonna be lurking in the shadows, keeping watch every minute. And if he so much as sullies, or stains, or soils the innocence of that angel who came straight from God, I swear to Sweet Jesus hanging out on the cross, I will mount his goddamn head on the grill of my four-by-four. I shit thee not. Do you, sir, understand me? It doesn't take much bad influence to ruin a woman. Case in point, that gargoyle who lives at the edge of the woods who I used to call my wife. I don't know what pushed her over the edge. I never saw it coming. I'll tell you one thing, now all those goddamn wind chimes make sense. She had the perfect life here. All she was required to do was sit in the comfort of the home I built, keep an eye on the kids, have my dinner ready, and keep her yapper shut. That's it! I barely even forced her to perform her Wifely Obligation, seeing as I was having it taken care of over at the club. Now, I'd call that pretty light lifting. But what are you gonna do? I never professed to understand women. I never professed to try to understand women. They're like handguns. You try to keep 'em clean. You try to keep 'em oiled. You take 'em out to the range every so often, fire 'em off. Then one day you forget to put the safety on, and when you're swabbing out the barrel, blammo, it goes off in your face. But I can't waste my energy thinking about women, I've got a town to run.

"And we are a town in trouble, no question about that. Our court case against the state is next week, and without a unified front, I just don't know how we stand a chance against them. Believe me, I'm in the government, and no one would stand a chance against me. Go ahead, call my bluff. I'd love it. If somebody wants to take me down, they'd better come in a group, and they'd better be carrying weapons. It won't be so easy to run me into an arsenic runoff containment tank. Anyway, I think we have a pretty strong case if only we can pull together. The government says they own the land we are on, as well as the dam. They say that they are well within their rights to tear it down.

"Okay, that's one for them. I'm sure the government sees us as a bunch of squatters who gradually accumulated at the bottom of a newly dry riverbed, and then in a response to rumors of the dam being torn down suddenly called themselves a town so that if the dam was torn down and the people were forced to move they would have to be financially compensated by the government. Well, that might be two for them. What they don't see is that we are a community with the remnants of a schoolhouse and a fire station! We are a hamlet of businesses and landfills and super-fund sites! And we are fathers, mothers, boys and girls, neighbors, friends, and corpses who are proud of our town of Wigfield! Yes, we may be small. Granted, not everybody has the proper dental records, but we will battle tirelessly to keep our town, and nothing will deter us! Our heels are dug in, and we are not going anywhere until the state can explain to us financially why we should leave, which we won't, ever! We just would like to hear their offer."

CHAPTER SEVENTEEN

THROUGH my many interviews with the people of Wigfield, a story was starting to shape up. I was certain of this. At this point I can't put my finger on exactly what that story might be, but it must be there. I felt that maybe I needed the other side of this story. Even though the thesis statement of this book, according to my editor, is the "disso-lution of America's small towns due to government interference or govern-ment disregard," my journalistic sense of fair play told me that Representative Bill Farber deserved the chance to give his side of the story, regardless of how many words that took. I decided to track him down. The time had come to look at the story coming straight from the gift horse's mouth, and regardless of where it might lead us, make him drink it!

I spied Representative Farber outside district court getting out of his car. He was a suspiciously normal-looking fellow in an oppressive gray suit. How could I land this interview? In the spirit of all the great investigative journal-ists, I tackled him in the street. Using the anger that clearly registered on his face to plot my next move, I quickly apologized by telling him I had mistaken him for an old rugby buddy of mine. After brushing the street debris from his suit, I quickly introduced myself to him and asked if I could briefly interview him for my book. He told me he was due in court, and this was a bad time. I assured him it would only take a moment and again apologized profusely, pointing out what a lucky accident this had been. He reluctantly agreed to give me a couple of minutes. We sat in the front seat of his car. I talked with Representative Farber about his desire to tear down the dam, upsetting tens of lives.

But first, here is some firsthand information that I learned secondhand through the rumor mill about the background of the representative. William J. Farber has been a state representative for eight years. He has a fat-cat family of three and a bureaucratic ranch-style home. While he proposes to destroy the town of Wigfield, he lives lavishly on his twenty-eight thousand dollars a year, handsomely supplemented by his wife's work with the physically handicapped.

Me: "First of all, Representative, thank you for taking the time to meet me in your car. I know this must be a very busy time of year for you and your Buick. Do you mind if I record our conversation?"

Farber: "No, not at all."

Me: "Do you have a tape recorder I can use?"

Farber: "I don't."

Me: "How about eight D-cell batteries? I'm out of juice."

Farber: "I'm sorry, I don't."

Me: "Great. I guess I'll just have to take notes. First of all, I know you've come under a lot of criticism by the people of this town

for your actions regarding the Bulkwaller Dam. I realize that this is probably only one side of the story. I'm hoping this interview can be a fair and open forum in which you can express your side of the story."

Farber: "I appreciate that."

Me: "Good. Question number one: Do you enjoy destroying lives?"

Farber: "I . . . don't understand your question."

Me: "I'll put down yes."

Farber: "Now, wait a second. First of all, Wigfield isn't a town. These people are living there illegally. It is an unincorporated illegal settlement on the dry bed of a former river and current illegal toxic dumping site. The scattered few who squat there have built ramshackle structures that violate every known ordinance of the fire code and would break numerous zoning violations if it were indeed an inhabitable zone, which it's not. Half of those people don't have social security numbers. They don't even have a zip code. They don't pay any taxes. They're not listed on any map. They're outside of any health care system or school district. Furthermore, there is only one way in and one way out of the entire—and I hesitate to use this word—town, which I believe makes the whole place a fire hazard. They get their electricity by jacking into power lines that run underneath the riverbed. The haphazard cluster of extension cords patched into this power line is not only a danger to the people who are there illegally, but is drawing valuable power from the hospital and fire departments in the neighboring town of Great Hope."

Me: "Have you ever been to a parade, Mr. Farber?"

Farber: "What?"

Me: "A parade, Mr. Farber! Have you ever applauded as the town beauty queen went by waving, perched on the back of a pesticide spray truck dressed up to look like a cannon? Have you ever had your heart warmed by the site of an infant winning a pie-eating contest?"

Farber: "I don't understand what this has to do with the dam issue."

Me: "Watch your language, sir!"

Farber: "I was referring to the Bulkwaller Dam."

Me: "Don't patronize me! I'm a journalist!"

Farber: "My point is, I don't understand what your questions about parades and pie-eating contests have to do with the issue of tearing down the dam."

Me: "I'm not surprised that you don't. Do you buy your tires used, Mr. Farber?"

Farber: "What?"

Me: "Your tires, Mr. Farber, are those the tires that came with the car?"

Farber: "No. I bought a new set about six months ago . . ."

Me: "I see. Can I read you something? This is a comment made by Burchal Sawyer, a resident in this town that you are so bent on destroying. He operates one of the used-tire lots that will be washed away when you tear down the dam. This is what he had to say:

I noticed his car parked on the street so I ran over to take a look at his tires. I did the penny test, where you see how much of the coin disappears in the groove of the tire, and frankly I was insulted by how much tread he has. I find it ironical that a black man has so much tread that you can't even see Lincoln's head.

How do you react to that, Mr. Farber?"

Farber: "I don't understand the significance. And anyway, if there were never new tires you couldn't have used ones!"

Me: "And if we didn't have dams you couldn't tear them down!"

Farber: "Look, that dam has no business being there. It was built by Alfonse T. Bulkwaller, whose family, incidentally, owned a concrete company. He built the dam for the sole purpose of charging the state for obscene amounts of concrete his family was selling at criminally inflated prices. He built the country's third-largest dam on top of what can best be described as a meandering creek. That dam provides no benefit. It provides no electricity and no irrigation."

Me: "It does provide one thing, Mr. Farber."

Farber: "What's that?"

Me: "Hope."

Farber: "Hope?"

Me: "Yes, Mr. Farber. Have you heard that word before, or is it not in your vocabulary? The children who play in its sun-drenched shadows look to this sleeping obelisk hoping it continues to watch over them, protecting them from the rushing water you are so intent on releasing."

Farber: "Look, I'm not trying to make anybody homeless. The state is willing to work with them to help them find alternative housing. Frankly, we don't even know who's there. They've never returned one single census form."

Me: "What about the homes that will be destroyed?!"

Farber: "Even though they have been built illegally on land that belongs to the state, we are willing to discuss a nominal relocation fee. But we are unwilling to give these people protection under the Eminent Domain Act. The state will not recognize this place as a town."

Me: "Well, I guess that will all be settled today in court."

Farber: "Hopefully. This has already taken way too much time away from my legislative duties."

Me: "Can you comment about the case?"

Farber: "I can't comment on the specifics, but I will say that the state is willing to abide by the judge's decision. The people of Wigfield don't have much of a case."

Me: "Well, Mr. Farber, as you know, I'm writing a book about this situation. I am merely an objective third party trying to record

the facts as they happen, but I would like to state, for the
record, that I hope you are served such a crushing defeat by
that judge that your wife is embarrassed to be seen in public
with you, and your children are taunted and then chased from
school by kids screaming 'Your daddy is a failure.' Thank you for
your time, and best of luck."

EIGHTEEN

CHAPTER EIGHTEEN

I'M sitting in the back of the courthouse as the hearing is about to begin. I recently learned something wonderful about our judicial system. I have to say, the idea of the American legal system being fair and impartial always rang a little hollow for me, considering the number of times I've woken up in handcuffs. I have never had much faith in the scales of Justice, as I am firmly convinced they will never tilt in my favor. But today my faith is restored, for I have just learned that if I ask for the court transcripts of this hearing, they have to give them to me, and I can then reprint them in my book . . . for free. Shine on, Lady Liberty, shine on.

Court Transcripts

September 07

Volume 3

PAGES 463–471

STATE DISTRICT COURT
FRESH SPRINGS RIVER COUNTY

Before the Honorable Eustis T. Coleman, Judge

Wigfield, *Plaintiff,* vs. Rep. Bill Farber, The State et al.; *Defendants.*	Fresh Springs River County Thursday, September 07

Transcripts of Proceedings

APPEARANCES:

For Plaintiff:

Fleet Hollinger

Charles Halstead

Burchal Sawyer

Hoyt Gein

For Defendants: Rep. Bill Farber

Thursday, September 07
8:48 A.M.

THE CLERK: Please rise for the Honorable Eustis T. Coleman.

JUDGE COLEMAN: Be seated. We have a motion filed by the town of Wigfield, August 14. At this time, the plaintiffs can make their opening statement.

MR. HOLLINGER
MR. SAWYER
MR. GEIN
MR. HALSTEAD: Judge . . . Our town . . . The loss of a way of life . . . Shut up . . . (unintelligible) . . . Fudgity fudgity . . . I must be recognized . . . Why . . . (unintelligible) . . . What happened to my pencil . . . You have a big mouth, Hollinger! (unintelligible) . . . My leg, Goddamnit . . .

JUDGE COLEMAN: Hold on! Gentlemen, please! I will not tolerate this behavior in my courtroom! First of all, I want to hear from one person at a time. Each of you identify yourselves so we know exactly who we are dealing with.

MR. HOLLINGER: Your Honor, I would like to apologize for my fellow . . . fellows. My name is Fleet Hollinger. I am the mayor of Wigfield.

MR. SAWYER: Yeah, right!

JUDGE COLEMAN: Who are you?

MR. SAWYER: Judge, my name is Burchal Sawyer and I am the mayor of Wigfield.

JUDGE COLEMAN: I'm sorry, Mr. Hollinger, what did you say your title was?

MR. HOLLINGER: The mayor of Wigfield.

MR. SAWYER: That is a bucket load of bullshit!

JUDGE COLEMAN: Your language, sir!

MR. SAWYER: Uhm . . . a heap of fudge?

MR. HALSTEAD: Fudge!

MR. HOLLINGER: Judge, I think it's pretty clear who is mayoral material here.

JUDGE COLEMAN: I've about had it, gentlemen!

MR. GEIN: Your Honor, if I may, I think I can clear this little matter up.

JUDGE COLEMAN: Who are you, another mayor?

MR. GEIN: That's very amusing, Judge, but no, I am Hoyt Gein, police chief under the mayor of Wigfield.

JUDGE COLEMAN: Which mayor, Mr. Gein? Mr. Hollinger or Mr. Sawyer?

MR. GEIN: Mr. Charles Halstead.

JUDGE COLEMAN: I've heard enough.

MR. SAWYER: Look, Judge, I don't even know how that 'tard got on the ballot!

MR. GEIN: He's more qualified than you!

MR. SAWYER: Who invited you, Gein?

MR. GEIN: I was invited by the adviser for Mayor Halstead for whom I am the spokesman and adviser!

JUDGE COLEMAN: Do you gentlemen have an opening statement or not?

MR. HOLLINGER: Yes, we do . . .

MR. SAWYER: Why should you read it, Hollinger?

MR. GEIN: I'd bet you two would burn like a gin-soaked hobo.

JUDGE COLEMAN: Mr. Gein, kindly put away those matches. Gentlemen, pick a single spokesman, understand?

MR. SAWYER: Can it be one of us?

JUDGE COLEMAN: That's the idea.

HOYT GEIN: Paper, scissors, stone!

JUDGE COLEMAN: I'll pick the spokesman. Mr. Hollinger, why don't you speak?

MR. HOLLINGER: Thank you, Your Honor, and may I compliment you on your choice.

JUDGE COLEMAN: Please make your statement.

MR. HOLLINGER: Your Honor, our scenic little town is nestled quaintly in the shadow of the Bulkwaller Dam. We are good people, Christians and pagans alike. For the record, we don't have any Jews.

MR. GEIN: Thanks in large part to my efforts.

MR. HOLLINGER: Our tiny little hamlet will soon be washed away by the cold, unforgiving waters of the so-called Fresh Springs River that the government in the person of Representative Bill Farber will be unleashing like a wolf upon her cubs.

JUDGE COLEMAN: So, you are saying you are opposed to the state tearing down the dam?

MR. HOLLINGER: Yes. And no . . .

JUDGE COLEMAN: I don't follow.

MR. HOLLINGER: There is a legal term that has come to our attention . . . oh hell, what's it called? Charlie, what was that thing you said?

MR. HALSTEAD: Fudge!

MR. HOLLINGER: No.

MR. HALSTEAD: I'm thirsty!

MR. HOLLINGER: That's not it, Charlie! Think!

MR. HALSTEAD: My pants are tight . . . I like shiny things . . . eminent domain . . .

MR. SAWYER: That's it!

MR. GEIN: Who's the 'tard now, Sawyer!

MR. HOLLINGER: Eminent domain! If residents are relocated by the state, they must be financially compensated for both home and property.

JUDGE COLEMAN: Yes, Mr. Hollinger, I know what eminent domain means. What's your point?

MR. HOLLINGER: The point is, Your Honor, we are never going to leave our homes. And by never, we mean until such time as we are fairly compensated for the pain of losing our hopes and dreams. The pain is immeasurable, as should be our compensation.

JUDGE COLEMAN: Mr. Farber, what do you have to say about all this?

MR. FARBER: Your Honor, eminent domain only applies to legally occupied incorporated towns. There is no precedent for payment to what really amounts to illegal squatters, no matter how many mayors they claim to have.

MR. HOLLINGER: How dare you?! Are you suggesting that we are merely posing as a town in order to get money when the dam is torn down? Does that even make sense?

MR. FARBER: Yes, it makes perfect sense. It's actually a fairly clever scam.

MR. SAWYER: Thank you.

JUDGE COLEMAN: Mr. Hollinger, do you, or any of the other . . . mayors possess articles of incorporation or a charter granted by the state board of commissioners?

MR. HOLLINGER: Yes we do, and what are they?

JUDGE COLEMAN: All right, I think we are done here.

(Disturbance from the gallery)

UNIDENTIFIED VOICE: Your Honor, my name is Russell Hokes, and I have something to say that is pertinent to this case.

JUDGE COLEMAN: All right, Mr. Hokes, speak, but I warn you, this had better relate directly to this case, or I will hold you in contempt.

MR. HOKES: I understand. As I said before, my name is Russell Hokes, and I am a writer who is writing a best-selling book about these people, and I think I know them better then they probably know themselves. Now, perhaps these people don't possess the necessary legal documents stating they are a town. And maybe they are unfamiliar with court proceedings and lack the experience required to prove their case, and Judge, perhaps their arguments are not based on rules or logic, or trial and error, or even properties of the universe. And maybe they didn't prepare by following lessons taught to them through history, or pay attention to instincts, or information in books. But I'll tell you this much, Judge: I have lived with these people for nearly two weeks now, talking to them, laughing with them, walking down their street, borrowing their money. I've sat in what used to be their diner. I've seen their children play on the mercury mound. I've sat in on town meetings. I have been to town funerals, and I think I can say with great confidence that if Wigfield is not a town, then I am not a writer! Thank you. I'll take my response off-air.

JUDGE COLEMAN: I am going to take this matter under consideration. The demolition of Bulkwaller Dam, proposed for October 18, is stayed for one month during which time this court will definitively determine the municipal status of Wigfield.

MR. HOLLINGER: Judge, I object!

JUDGE COLEMAN: To what?

MR. HOLLINGER: To the things you are saying?

JUDGE COLEMAN: Do you understand what I'm saying?

MR. HOLLINGER: I guess that's the source of my objection.

JUDGE COLEMAN: I am not allowing the state to tear down the dam for one month. You will have that one month to prove you are a town. If you can prove you are a town in that time, the state will be forced to compensate you under the Eminent Domain Act should the state continue with its planned demolition of the dam. If you can't prove your township, the dam may come down and the state will have no financial obligation to you whatsoever.

MR. HOLLINGER: Judge, I object!

JUDGE COLEMAN: To what?

MR. HOLLINGER: Why do we have to prove we're a town? Mr. Farber doesn't have to prove he's a representative.

JUDGE COLEMAN: He is an elected official! Look, gentlemen, I am giving you a gift. The choice is yours. Because you have no paperwork stating you are a town I can throw out your motion right now and allow the state to tear down the dam without any compensation for Wigfield, or you can take the month I offered and prove to this court that you are indeed a town. What's it going to be?

MR. HOLLINGER: In light of the things you are saying I guess my response is: Objection overruled.

NINETEEN

CHAPTER NINETEEN

O**NE** month! The judge has made it clear, Wigfield has one month to prove it is a town, but which month? In the hardworking can-do stick-to-itiveness that is the hallmark of the American small town, Wigfield chose the month immediately following the ruling. But what can be achieved in a twelfth of a year? That's thirty days to you and me, unless of course it's February. Well, we all know the well-worn adage:

Thirty days hath December,
June, July and remember,
If you're in a different month,
That hath less then thirty-oneth,
Chances are it's February,
A month in which you must be wary
Not to count to thirty days,
'Cause less than that it has always,
But not so few as twenty-seven,
That can't be, oh no my heaven,
Unless it is the year that leaps

For always one more day it keeps

To tag upon the twenty-eight

To keep the calendar up to date.

In a hastily thrown together assemblage, the town residents accumulated in groups of clumps at the newly designated town hall, which, until a few hours ago, was a town morgue. There was a certain simple poetry to the setting. Live town members meeting alongside dead town members. Living residents shouting out suggestions while the dead ones kept a respectful silence. At first the town struggled for a solution, then they clamored for an answer, finally settling for a result. The early suggestions showed promise but sadly no potential.

"Add the words, *Town of* to the Wigfield sign," suggested someone from the crowd.

"Get a Wigfield sign," said another.

"Take Bill Farber out!" was lobbed from the back and hailed by the mob.

"Construct an ancient wonder! Think pyramid!" an excited voice offered.

"Kidnap Farber's family!" was warmly received.

But none of the fine ideas seemed effortless enough to sway the majority of the proud but tired Wigfieldeans. It wasn't their intellect or imagination that was limited, but rather their task was limitless. Because what is a town? How can it be defined? Well, the *American Standard Dictionary* has this to say, and I plagiarize directly . . .

town (toun) *n.* **1. a.** *Abbr.* **t. T. tn.** An incorporated settlement, larger than a village and smaller than a city. **b.** The inhabitants of such a settlement.

This seemed to be a reasonable definition. Succinct? Yes. Clear? Absolutely. But was it in-depth enough? More important, was it in-length enough? I decided that even though it was an American word, I would give the English a chance to chime in, for they usually have something to say. I turned to the *Cambridge Definitive* . . .

> **town**/taːn/ *noun* **1.** populated area, its size being somewhere between a city and a village. **2.** The main city of a populated area. **3.** the people that comprise said population center. EX: *The blokes who lived in the flat finished their bangers and mash, turned off the telly and took the lift down to the pavement in order to queue for the tram just like the rest of the bloody town.*

Cheerio, my foreign friends. A definition that is forty-eight words more concise than our timid chums over at *American Heritage*. But could this really be the last word, or words, on "town"? Something, specifically my contract, told me that one Mr. Marion Webster might have something to say . . .

> **town** Pronunciation: 'taŭn
>
> Function: noun
> Etymology: Mid to low English, from Old English *tūn*, group, bunch, weapon; akin to Late low High Swiss/Deutsch *zūn*, oppressive enclave (literally); place where leather shorts are considered appropriate dress. Old Irish town; town
> Date: before 4th century
> **1.** a cluster or clump of groups called a town: See town
> **2.** a group of prairie dog burrows
>
> **—on the town:** to pursue entertainment or amusement (as city nightlife) especially as a relief from routine; **to town around:** to act in a humorous fashion like a town; **what goes around comes to**

> **town** the belief that the energy a person puts out will show back up
> in a populated area uninvited

Yes! A whopping 106 words! Now that is a definition I can sink my tooth into! It appears the Brits have been bested again! Sorry, King George, old chap! I don't know what you people are doing over at Webster, but keep it up!

But ultimately, any definition of a town is meaningless, especially three of them, because a town is more than just a number of words on a paper, even if that number is 438. (438!) A town is a feeling. Much like the feeling the modern-day folk-rock troubadour John Mellencamp, aka John Cougar, aka John Cougar Mellencamp, aka Mellencamp, captured in his song "Small Town," which I would have liked to reproduce in its entirety, but due to copyright constraints I cannot. I can tell you this much, the words *small town* are used eighteen times! The same words—eighteen times in one song! (He must have the same unreasonable contract I do.) The point is, in songs you can repeat the same words over and over again and no one bats an eye, but for some reason, because this is a book, my editor tells me I'm supposed to make each sentence mean something different! You figure it, 'cause frankly, I am all yelled out about it.

Town. How do you measure the idea of town? What makes a town a town? Town? Sure, there are the obvious things—a chamber of commerce, a school system, a viable health care facility—but the residents of Wigfield were searching for something a little more tangible.

But what? I realize my duty as a documentarian. I am supposed to be the eyes in the wall, the ear to the ground. An unnoticeable nonparticipant. A friendly ghost. Much like those missionaries of yesteryear who would travel to the deepest parts of the Darkest Continent to observe the natives without upsetting the balance of the tribe. I, too, am here to remain unobtrusive.

So I don't know what came over me when, during the town meeting, I rose to my feet and from my obscurity shouted the word *Parade!* Silence overtook the quiet room as the eyes turned and focused on my lips. My heart sank, my palms sweated, as their ears perked to the utterance of my tongue . . . "Parade?" I mumbled triumphantly. Almost immediately, like a cannon shot, a faint murmur began to brew among the crowd. "Parade," they began to utter, until the excitement swept through the room, like a glacier overtaking a continent. After the idea was thoroughly mulled, it seemed obvious. What better way to prove you are something you are not than to celebrate the very thing that someone says you aren't! And what better way to celebrate than with a parade?

Parades have long been associated with small towns. Most small-town residents, at the drop of a hat, are willing to take to the streets holding balloons or flags or weapons and march in the same direction, and when they do, you can be sure a crowd will gather. I suppose academics over the years have tried to explain the popularity of parades using fancy technical words and phrases, like "Parades are when people march together to celebrate something" or "A parade is a festive procession." But it boils down to the simple fact that people love to watch people doing stuff, and people love to be watched by other people while they do stuff. That's it plain and simple.

Historically, the first parades predated all the latter parades, which gave them an advantage in establishing what the traditions would be. Usually, these early parades consisted of mobs of torch-wielding townspeople chanting festive slogans like "Kill the monster" as they searched through swamps for the misunderstood reanimated hulking creature. So popular were these gatherings that soon they were sanctioned by the town burgermeister, and floats and alcohol were added. Today, modern parades consist of a variety of charming elements familiar to us all, such as a carload of fresh faced giggling cheerleaders whose pleated skirts flutter in the breeze; the local beauty queen proudly displaying her sash draped over her heaving, ample, prize-winning bosom(s); the dairy princess in her lederhosen and dirndl, her torso cinched tight, her milky white arms swaying like willow branches as she waves to the mesmerized onlookers; the majorette in thigh-high white leather boots, goose-stepping like a proud pony who needs to be broken, waving her baton like a schoolmarm switching the backside of a naughty boy. And, of course, balloons.

But like snakes in a rope factory, there were naysayers amongst the assemblage who caviled,* How much attention would one parade generate? Doubt threatened to strangle my brainchild in the incubator.

But then it hit me like a violent felon: "One parade won't help, but one continuous parade might!" We will take to the streets of Wigfield and not rest from our march until we are recognized as having the right to be here!

Fleet Hollinger put the matter to the floor and with a vote of fourteen against, seventeen for, it was unanimous: Wigfield would walk back and forth in front of one another until it made some sort of point!

---

*I am including the word *cavil* under protest, which I officially register now. My editor, who seems overly concerned with what words end up in my book, assured me it was appropriate here. Who knows, I'm not taking the time to look it up. I have a book to write. 12,586 words left to be exact.

CHAPTER TWENTY

As parade day approached, I decided to wander the village and talk to some of the potential paraders. I hoped to get a temperature reading as to how high the fever pitch was running and whether it was contagious.

THE GRIMMETTS

Eleanor: "We love parades!"

Udell: "Love 'em. Hasn't been one around here for ten years."

Eleanor: "Oh, longer than that . . ."

Udell: "No. Remember it was dark, Hoyt threw that thing together at the last minute, we paraded up to the gorge . . ."

Eleanor: "Oh, that was no parade. It was a lynching . . ."

Udell: "Right, you're right. Ugly business, that."

Eleanor: "What's best about a small-town parade is that everybody knows everybody else."

Udell: "You know, people will say, 'Why, there's young Dillard Rankin pushing his mother in a wheelchair!' "

Eleanor: "She doesn't need to use that chair. She walks as good as I do."

Udell: "I know."

Eleanor: "She just has to stay in the chair until the insurance case is settled."

Udell: "Or you might say, 'There's Raven! I've seen her naked!' "

Eleanor: "Udell!"

Udell: "I'm talking about what people might say. Not me. Point is, at parades you get to see things you don't usually get to see outside the confines of a strip club."

Eleanor: "Like large groups of people walking together while other people watch."

Udell: "Right. Anyway, we're excited! We realize that this is our last chance. If this parade doesn't work, it looks likely that me and Eleanor here are going to have to pack up and hit the road with empty pockets."

Eleanor: "Yesterday afternoon I had a nightmare that they exploded the dam while we were still trying to pack. The whole town turned into a lake. I was swimming along the top, with all our furniture floating around, and I was calling out for Udell. I was worried because I know he can't swim because of his condition."

Udell: "It's not a condition, Eleanor! It's just a minor nuisance."

Eleanor: "It's a condition, Udell."

Udell: "While I was working at the plant, I started to notice that my . . . manhood was starting to swell a bit and it was turning a little purple. And now, well, my ballsack looks like an eggplant. Sometimes I'm tempted to bread it."

Eleanor: "Udell!"

Udell: "Just tryin' to keep it light. The point is, we were never able to have kids, but we tried. Came pretty close a few times."

Eleanor: "We're talking about the parade here, Udell."

Udell: "There is nothin' to be ashamed of, Eleanor. There was one time she managed to pop something out. Threw us for a loop for a while."

Eleanor: "I carried it nineteen months. I was sure we had a winner."

Udell: "Jesus, it was strong."

Eleanor: "Charlie . . ."

Udell: ". . . mean as hell."

Eleanor: "Charlie."

Udell: "I'm uncomfortable giving it a name."

Eleanor: "I used to feed him."

Udell: "Eleanor . . ."

Eleanor: "I *did*. Right in the mouth."

Udell: "It was an eye."

Eleanor: "It was a mouth."

Udell: "All I know is when you tried to feed it there, it would wink at you."

Eleanor: (weeping softly)

Udell: "It eventually . . . uh . . . broke free. Ran off into the night. Haven't seen it since. Well, we hear rumors."

Eleanor: "Oh, I don't believe those."

Udell: "I don't know . . ."

Eleanor: "He wouldn't hurt anyone. Someday I hope he comes back home . . . during the daylight."

Udell: "He'd like a parade . . ."

THEA

"Oh, a parade! You know the whole genesis of parades harkens back to the processions of the Goths and the druidic overlords of pre-Christian Normandy, I speak of course of the Celts, who in their transpagan new moon celebration would choose a male virgin who would then be hoisted on a pike into the boughs of a mallorn tree, then, using a golden scythe, they would harvest the mistletoe and anoint his body with its berries before they eviscerated him in obeisance to Cthulu, the lord of chaos, in obviation of their sins. They would then feast upon his privates. Anyway, sounds like a good time, Amythys and I will be there."

MAE ELLA PADGETT

"Parade? A parade to save the town? I don't like it. I used to live in Freak Town just outside of Sarasota. I had a nice little bungalow, roomed with Bobo the Flame-Throwing Dwarf, and Wolf Boy, who later became known as Wolf Man, and even later, for one brief final performance, Flaming Wolf Man, thanks to an argument with Bobo. I lived right next door to the Human Blockhead. I used to do patter for the Crocodile Twins. You know, 'Back, back, back in time! See them transformed from the primordial stew! They walk, they talk, they crawl on their bellies like a reptile, no photographs, no papier-mâché, they are *alive*! Please, no infants, no elderly, no breast-feeding mothers, your milk may curdle in the teat! The Crocodile Twins . . . they are *alive*!'"

"Anyway, times got pretty rough in Freak Town due to the year of the hard freeze, which wiped out most of the citrus crop, you know, migrant workers were a large part of our audience. Anyway, we needed to drum up some cash. We decided to go back to the basics. Mr. Ripley once said to me in a dream, 'Go with what you know,' so we decided to pound the pavement in what we delicately called The Freak Parade. This was surefire, we thought. Sure, it's a lot of legwork for the freaks. Sure, admittedly there was a healthy dose of taunting and occasional rock throwing by the local clergy. But a buck's a buck, and nobody understands that more than a freak merchant. So we hit the road. And guess what? It was a miserable failure. We started in small towns, but there wasn't much of a turnout, perhaps people have lost their stomachs for freaks, I don't know. So, anyway, I decided we needed to parade somewhere a little more prominent. I figured we should go down this beautiful stretch of I-75 between Tallahassee and Tampa Bay. Cody was supposed to arrive before us and cone off a slice of the freeway. Apparently Cody had other priorities, but we decided to parade anyway. A few moments after we started, disaster struck when a double-wide manure spreader came around a blind corner, jackknifed, and took out most of the freaks, slapping them off the road like a windshield wiper. We picked up what was left of them with dabs of cotton. Shortly thereafter I bid a hasty adieu to Freak Town. I guess my point is, I lost a pretty penny on that parade, and you know what they say, once burned, twice shy."

CARLA PORT HOLLINGER

"What do I think about the parade? I mean, I don't care, whatever. I don't know if I'll even go. My mom is gonna be there with her stupid witch outfit, you know, flowing robe, spangled thong, and those pagan curly-toed goatskin slippers with the sheep-hoof heels. It's so embarrassing. What do I care? I hardly talk to my mom anymore anyway. Sometimes I visit her at her cave, which isn't really a cave—it's just a trailer home that got halfway buried in a mud slide. I don't go over there much, cuz Mom is always on me about going on one of her Menstrual Jamborees. What a joke. It's so queer. I'm sorry, but I just don't want to dance around a bonfire and paint pictures with my menstrual blood—my mom calls it the 'unholy nectar'—or use a sea sponge as a tampon. Whatever.

"And regardless of what my so-called mother says, I am not afraid of my vagina. Though it seems like some other people around here are. I heard about Dillard Rankin and his supposed preengagement to Regina Cox. What a joke. I really don't care about any of it. I so don't care that I don't care what I'm saying right now. You know what I'm saying? Regina Cox! What a joke! You know what we call her? Vagina. Vagina Cox. That's what we used to call her. Me and Amythys. Amythys . . . what a joke. She and my mom do everything together. She thinks she's so cool now because she's a witch apprentice. Well, I happen to know that her real name is not Amythys. That's just what my mom calls her for business reasons. Her real name is Judy Brown, and we used to go to school together. We used to call her Doody Brown. Me and Regina. Anyway, the three of us don't speak anymore. Anyway, who wants to go to a parade and watch Dillard and Vagina walk around together? I mean, I guess I do, 'cause I so don't care.

"Will you be talking to Dillard? Could you give him this poem for me? But please don't read it or show it to anyone, cuz I would just die. It's too personal."

The following is a full reprint of the poem:

DILLARD

I am a bird on a branch

Who watches you walk in the parade below

You Unknowing that the Rustle from above is not of the leaves

But the quivering of my feathers stirred by the pounding of my heart

Falling around you like petals in your path

I would fly to your shoulder and nest in your hair all summer

Take shelter from the rain behind your earlobe

Fan you from the heat with my wings

Then in winter migrate south to your tropical sanctuary

Please become a bird like me.

I cannot fly free without your love

I am caged

Caged within your ribs

Your rib's cage.

Regina Cox is so two-faced,

I'd love to peck her four eyes out.

CINNAMON

"I think it's a wonderful idea! The girls and I put on a parade for the customers every night, and the crowd loves it, and so do we! It's the only time of the night all us girls get to wear our full costumes! All the costumes look great, because it's before the customers begin to paw at them and your feather boa gets all gummed up. Anyway, the dj plays something upbeat and we march in line in and out of the tables. The crowd likes to yell encouragements like 'Shake your tits!' and 'Show us your tits!' and 'I want to paw at your tits.' It's really a lot of fun."

CHAPTER TWENTY-ONE

Reprinted from the *Wigfield Sporadic.*

GRAND PARADE STARTS TODAY!

By ENNIS CHISOLM

WIGFIELD, Oct. 7th—The townspeople of Wigfield will celebrate the Town-hood of their Town today with a continuous parade through the center of Town.

Town of Wigfield to Hold Marathon Parade

The kickoff point will be in front of Fleet Hollinger's Auto Parts and the happy throng will then proceed along the designated parade route past Tit Time Show Palace and Sawyer's Used Auto Parts Headquarters and Graveyard Emporium, on to the Twat Shop and the Rigid Squirrel, thence toward The Bacon Strip and the Topless Car Wash, the Topless Ten-Minute Oil Change, and the All-Nude Fix-a-Flat. Following this passing of the first part of the passage, they will then amble in front of Abra-cadavre's Morgue and Gentlemen's Club (formerly Croak-us Poke-us) until they complete the journey in front of the Library of Cumgress. All in all, a journey of nearly 400 yards. They will then turn and repeat as necessary. So get there early and get there often to pick a spot because the parade won't last forever, just a really long time.

First Day of Parade a Rousing Success!

By ENNIS CHISOLM

WIGFIELD, Oct. 9th—The Town of Wigfield celebrated its heritage in a time-honored manner yesterday with a parade. There was fun for all!

At a bright and early 1:30 in the afternoon, the resident who was not marching in the parade lined the route as the floats started their engines. First up was Donnie Larson driving the Tit Time Float—a flatbed truck loaded with Working Gals—Shy-anne, Ginger Snaps, CJ, Raven, Micky, and Pebbles. The crowd was receptive and generous with his applause. Next came the Honorable Mayors. All three were in the spirit of the moment, especially Mayor Halstead, who waved frantically from the confines of his protective harness. Chief Gein was in firm control of Mayor Halstead at all times.

The highlight of the parade had to be Julian Childs's "Salute to Cabaret." Elaborately decorated in crepe paper with flashing lights and a rumored 15,000 individually applied rose petals, Childs thrilled the crowd. His float was also festive.

One of the most heartwarming moments of the parade came as Mae Ella Padgett was honored as the Oldest Person in Town, while Dottie Fore was hailed as the Most Elderly. Both women seemed equally weathered.

Local cut-up Lenare Degroat won First Prize for Originality with his "Bone Float," a float made entirely of bones. Leading this reporter to ask, "Hey, Lenare, where'd you get all those bones?" A brief altercation ensued.

The parade continues tonight and into tomorrow and onward for the foreseeable future. Let's all wish ourselves Good Luck as we march on to further marching!

MAYORS PLEAD, THREATEN PARADE VOLUNTEERS

By ENNIS CHISOLM

WIGFIELD, Oct. 11th—Mayor Fleet Hollinger today called on local paraders to "not abandon the route" as exhaustion thinned the ranks of the celebration. The plea was received with mixed enthusiasm. Longtime bachelor/actor Julian Childs typified the response.

"My haunches are numb, my rabbits are frazzled, my nerves are shot, and my roses are wilting. I need a break."

But others in the procession were more adamant. Area dancer Cinnamon responded more positively to the march. "Has it been that long? I'm dizzy."

Mae Ella Padgett spoke for many of the older residents of Wigfield when she said that "these kids today don't know the first thing about walking back and forth. I could do it for days as long as I was riding on a float."

Meanwhile, the march goes on. Parade Security, Billy and Jackie Barnhiesel, work the crowd with truncheons to keep spirits light. Mayor Fleet Hollinger has been there 24 hours a day in spirit.

Parade Slows to Crawl

By ENNIS CHISOLM

WIGFIELD, Oct. 12th—As the first annual Wigfield Parade Day entered its fifth day today, exhaustion took a heavy toll on the proud but humble residents as well as on the floats.

Enthusiasm Turns to Tragedy

The Tit Time float was commandeered by club manager/patron Donnie Larson, who lost control of the "celebratory Juggernaut" and careened into Lenare Degroat's festive "Wagon of Doom." Bewildered strippers and shards of bone shrapnel tore through the unsuspecting crowd, which consisted mostly of weary marchers. Donnie Larson had this to say:

"I know as well as anybody there that I should not have been behind the wheel of that rig. I knew it. You knew it. The girls knew it. Frankly, I'm just as angry as you are. And I'm all for finding out whose idea it was that I drive and punishing that person to the full extent of the law will allow. I, and I include me in this, should be removed from our highway system and my driving privileges should be ceased. That is common knowledge. And I'll say that to anybody."

Mayor Fleet Hollinger captured the mood, "I'd be the last one to tell anybody to stop, but let me be the first to say this has got to end."

Based on the weary faces of the once energetic marchers, it would appear that this Parade for Township has come to an end, well short of its mark.

GUEST EDITORIAL BY RUSSELL HOKES

Marchers, Dreams in Shambles

WIGFIELD, Oct. 12th—Our little walk has had a glorious run, but it looks like the push for township has come to an end. It's a dark day in a town that never was but could've been if only it were to be. Over the thunderous footfalls of doom one can hear the pitter-patter of the many little feet of the tiny grim reapers who are descending on our area, scythes aloft to shear away the tenuous foundations that this town is not built upon and never will be.

Our Parade has been much akin to the marches of the civil rights era. With one key difference: no black people. But still their charming chant rings as true here today as it did all those years ago. We Shall Overcome. With one other key difference. We won't.

So there goes the neighborhood. It's been a battle royal, this barn burner, this clash of the Titans, and we fought like cornered rats until the last dog was hung and the cows were coming home to roost, but it is time to throw in the towel and call a spade a spade—the fat lady is singing, it's all over but the shoutin', 'cause when you're in a hole you stop digging and smell the roses that, like the spoils, will go to the victor. And here's a thought like a bolt from the blue: This could all be a blessing in disguise, a gift from the gods, a kick in the backside if you will. It certainly is one for the books that beggars belief. We were caught napping with our pants down. You win some you lose some, pays your money and takes your chances. But just when it gets darkest before the dawn, and you need a little Christmas, right this very minute, remember this: Quitters never win and neither do losers, and you people are both.

CHAPTER TWENTY-TWO

OCT. 19, WIGFIELD TOWN MEETING

Please note the seven-day gap.

But why a seven-day gap in a book that has slavishly held to a chronological order, a book completely devoted to cataloging the minutia of my day-to-day life in Wigfield no matter how insignificant? Perhaps I did it to create dramatic tension. My detractors, of whom I have many, would have you believe I left town like some fair-weather rat jumping from a sinking friend, only to return once I read in a distant city newspaper that Wigfield's fate was suddenly looking up. Well maybe I did pack up everything I own including a few things I didn't. Perhaps I borrowed the Grimmetts' car on a semipermanent basis, pushing the vehicle to the edge of town during the blackness of night and then starting it when out of earshot. And yes, let's say for argument's sake I did drive south to a border town and attempt to pawn some ladies' jewelry. The point is this: I am not some fly-by-night tapeworm leaving a cooling corpse. The fact of the matter is/was I needed to clear my head. I needed to get some distance from my subject and if possible from myself in order to preserve my objectivity. I love Wigfield that much, so much, that I was/am willing to abandon her at her darkest hour. It is sheer coincidence that my return coincided with Wig-field's miraculous turnaround. More about that a hundred words from now. But first, if I may, I'd like to express how exciting it is for me to be back in the saddle, and it's true what they say about bicycles, you can never forget them, and it's never been more evident than in my ability to pick up from where I left off with the same dedication to craftsmanship that I have previously demonstrated heretofore, hither, and henceforth. I know you can't wait to hear about what happened after the horrible accident that turned around the town of Wigfield, so I'm just going to jump in here at word number ninety-nine.

As you know, based on my cunning suggestion, Wigfield decided to hold a nonstop Protest Parade Strike. Spirits were high and so was the turnout. The first few days were high energy and closely resembled a parade. After day three, things took a turn for the ugly. Townspeople were becoming increas-ingly weary and angry. There was a looming threat that the ranks would break. Of all the marchers, my frustration was perhaps the greatest as I was unable to march due to my hip joints (continuous walking occasionally aggravates my coccyx). Nevertheirregardless, I kept watching. Why couldn't they keep marching? I even accused certain members of the procession of trying to sab-otage my idea. I'm well aware how jealousy can corrupt the mind. Then it dawned on me: All that was needed was a little sleep. A rest for the weary. I was right. In the morning, I felt refreshed. After a hearty breakfast, I strolled back to the parade, shocked to find the marchers as exhausted as I was rein-vigorated. Mayor Hollinger attempted to keep the marchers motivated, but eventually even a horse doesn't respond to the crop. These people were clearly on their last leg.

But even severe fatigue doesn't explain what happened next. A bleary-eyed Donnie Larson inexplicably lost control of his float, ramming into Lenare Degroat. I don't want to go into the details of the grisly aftermath. I'm not some journalistic vulture who swoops down on the decaying meat of someone else's sorrow in the hopes of profiting. I can assure you, in my book you will not see phrases such as: jumbled piles of body parts, chunks of bone, blood-soaked concrete, or scattered hunks of brains. I don't operate that way. We all can imagine what an accident scene looks like, I'm talking about a real stomach turner, without having it spelled out. Now I know six times out of ten the violent mangling of innocent paraders is going to seem catastrophic, but this occasion was different.

What happened next is almost impossible to believe, but here goes: Because of the accident, a county police report was filed and posted in the daily police blotter. A reporter at one of the big-city papers picked it up and wrote a human-interest story about the travails of Wigfield that I'm sure I will be accused of plagiarizing, an accusation I vehemently deny. You couldn't pay me enough to plagiarize it. First off, it completely failed to capture the plight of disappearing small towns. How could it? It was only 240 words long. I'm 40, 240 words in and I haven't even come close.

Here was his "headline."

Small Town Parades to Save Self

That's flashy! (Sarcasm)

Anyway, somehow that story piqued the interest of other newspapers. Soon, they began showing up in Wigfield, curious to see "the small town endlessly parading to save itself." Stories began to spread like syphilis at summer camp, and before long crowds began to show up along the parade route. Thanks to their newfound celebrity and massive doses of amphetamines, the marchers found a third wind lurking deep within their second winds. They cleaned up the parade route and hit the pavement again. All this publicity created a backlash of support and before you could say "incorporate," the masses were screaming about "the poor little town that is going to be destroyed by the state." As a result, I'm anticipating that Representative Farber will announce that he is not tearing down the dam. Could it be? Perhaps it's not so easy to destroy a town in full view of the rest of the state. What's the matter, Representative? Getting cold feet? Representative Farber has informed the town that he would like to address them today. I practiced my gloat in the mirror, and then headed over to the meeting.

(Tape Transcripts)

I sit in on this town meeting with rapt eagerness. It's impossible to conceive, after the way things looked the morning of October 12, that the situation could turn around so abruptly, and so in our favor. Representative Bill Farber is here, and is planning to make a statement.

FLEET HOLLINGER: All right, people. Listen up. Thanks for coming to the town meeting. I know everybody is pretty excited, but let's try and keep a cap on it. Everybody is gonna get what's coming to 'em, so relax. Now, let's get this show on the road.

DOTTIE FORE: Can we turn the heat up in here?

HOLLINGER: I'm not gonna tell you again, Dottie, it's a morgue. If it gets above forty the bodies start to turn. Bring a sweater next time. Here's the deal. Representative Bill Farber . . . Hey! That's uncalled for, he's turning out to be one of the good ones, and we should encourage that because they're few and far between. Anyway, Representative Bill Farber is here to say a few words. I think we'll all be very interested. Let's give him our undivided attention. Mr. Farber, you have the floor.

BILL FARBER: Thank you. Well, ladies and gentlemen, what I have to say is very simple, really. You win.

(Screams, hoots, and hollers)

BURCHAL SAWYER: Hot damnation!

HOLLINGER: OK, OK. Calm down folks.

SAWYER: I'll take it in cash, Farber! And if you don't mind, I'll take it now!

(More cheers)

FARBER: Take what?

HOLLINGER: Well, I think what Mr. Sawyer is referring to is our eminent domain money. Our compensation for all that we will lose.

FARBER: But that's what I'm saying. You don't lose. You win. The state is bowing to public pressure and has decided not to tear down the Bulkwaller Dam.

(Cheering from me)

HOLLINGER: Tear it down or don't tear it down, I don't give a damn, as long as you pay up.

FARBER: I don't think you understand. The state is not obligated to pay compensatory damages if no such damages occur.

HOLLINGER: I understand. So, what does that break down to per person?

FARBER: Zero. The state is giving you no money.

(Murmurs from the audience)

HOLLINGER: Come again?

MAE ELLA PADGETT: Where's our money?

(A chant of "Where's our money" rings out from the floor and begins to build.)

FARBER: None of you are getting any money. Not from me, and not from the state. No money. Nothing.

SAWYER: You liar! What's in that big brown envelope?

FARBER: I'm glad you asked. I don't have any money for you, but I do have your new town charter that was granted by the county commissioners late last night, officially incorporating the municipality of Wigfield. Here you are, Mr. Hollinger.

(Silence)

Oh, by the way, you should note that among the responsibilities that come with townhood are providing proper sewage, streetlights, a school system, a water filtration plant . . . well, the list goes on. A tax will have to be levied on the citizens and businesses to pay for all that, of course. You have until the first of the year to initiate these actions.

HOLLINGER: What if we don't?

FARBER: Well, in that case, the town will be dissolved, your property confiscated without compensation, you will all be forcibly removed from the area, and all town officials, which I might remind you are legally listed as Hollinger, Sawyer, Gein, and Halstead, will be subject to criminal prosecution.

HOLLINGER: Uh huh . . .

FARBER: Which would most likely result in lengthy jail terms. Good luck, Misters Mayor, and congratulations.

(Author's note: Yes! Victory! I speak this into the microphone at a feverish pace in attempts to keep up with the excitement of the moment! I'm sure the newly minted town of Wigfield will want to offer me their gratitude, and I accept. It was a hard fight, but together I managed to pull it off. As Bill Farber exits, hiding his defeat behind a mischievous grin, the town members of Wigfield sit silent, seemingly unable, for the moment, to comprehend the good fortune that has just been bestowed upon them.)

JULIAN CHILDS: What are we going to do now?

SAWYER: Well, I think we need to turn that over to Mr. Hollinger, because I regret to inform you that I have resigned my third of the mayorship.

HOLLINGER: What are you talking about, Burchal?

SAWYER: Who we kiddin', Fleet, you're the right man for the job. Everybody knows it.

HOLLINGER: It's too late to resign.

SAWYER: Well, I already resigned before the meeting started, I only waited until now to make it official because I didn't want to put a damper on the festivities. So all I have to say is, it's been my pleasure serving as one of the mayors, I wouldn't have missed it for anything, and I'm sure gonna miss it. Good luck.

HOLLINGER: You're not going anywhere, Sawyer. According to these legal documents, you are one of the mayors, and nothing is going to change that.

SAWYER: Listen, you son of a bitch, you were leading in the polls when the fire broke out! Isn't that what you said? And what about droolie over here, why don't we just make him the mayor? What do you say, Halstead? Or should I say Gein?

HOYT GEIN: Don't look at me. You can make him whatever you want. Make him emperor, what do I care, he fired me this afternoon.

HOLLINGER: Listen, nobody is going anywhere. I'm not going down alone. We're all in this together, whether you like it or not.

SAWYER: You don't control me! Out of my way!

HOLLINGER: Get your hands off me, Sawyer, you little shit!

(Sounds of scuffling)

FORE: He's killing him! He's killing him! Get out of my way! I can't see!

CHILDS: There is no reason for violence! I demand this stop until I've had the opportunity to exit safely.

PADGETT: I'm throwing my chair! Wheeee . . . !

TWENTY-THREE

CHAPTER TWENTY-THREE

OCT. 23

Please note additional four-day gap.

This book is currently operating at a cumulative eleven-day gap. I want to assure you that the most recent gap was out of my control and, in an unforeseen unfortunate addition, has clouded my memory. I can't say that I'm fully recovered. I can't say I can tell you what hit me. I can say my skull will never be the same. I'm still a bit in the dark about what I last remember as perhaps the greatest triumph in municipal history turning into a sudden and horrible melee. I'm doing my best to untangle the morass of memories that have badly decomposed during my latest coma, but so far I'm unable to reconstruct a coherent scenario.

So, in light of the darkness, I offer these secondhand first-person accounts of what happened.

MAE ELLA

"Well, when you've lived as long as I have, you've seen everything, but I never saw this coming down the pike. I can't believe Farber turned on us like that. I feel cold-cocked. I feel like I was hit with a blind-side roundhouse haymaker sucker punch. I'm a little angry. This is a lot like Pearl Harbor, except instead of the menace being yellow it's a more chocolaty color. After the donnybrook broke out when Farber dropped that bomb on us, I thought it was all over. Apparently some hothead, I'm not saying it was me, tossed some folding chairs into the fray to drive home a point that escapes me now and maybe was a little uncalled for. I will say that you, Hokes, must have a skull made out of sponge cake. Anyway, one of the steel corners of another chair I didn't throw kind of caught a glancing blow off Lenare's eye socket, and as we all know, Lenare has a bit of a short fuse. Well, actually, he has no fuse, he's pretty much all bomb. I'm an old woman, the oldest in town, so I got the hell out of there. I have to tell you, I didn't become the oldest woman in town by staying in a room full of knives. The rest of what I know is pretty much hearsay. You know, second- and third-party stuff, nothing that would hold up in a court of law, so there is no need to subpoena me.

"After I left, I guess the fat really hit the grease fire. Burchal Sawyer's chest just happened to be standing between Lenare's knife and the wall that Lenare was holding him against. He'll bounce back, it's not the first time his chest has tasted steel. After that point, the violence started to escalate. Fleet called upon the crowd-control talent of the Barnhiesel twins, Billy and Jackie. Based on the fracture patterns on some of the skulls I've seen, I'd guess they used steel pipes. Someone fleeing the area said those whistling pipes slamming against rib cages sounded like somebody pounding out a veal cutlet with a bassoon. And then things got ugly, there is no other word for it. In a move to calm the panicked and fleeing townsfolk, Fleet Hollinger had his boys chain the doors shut. Then Hoyt Gein, in an attempt to . . . I'm not sure what he was attempting to do—no one really knows— from someplace produces a torch, well, not so much a torch as a snapped-off broom handle with some rags tied around one end that were soaked in acetone. He then starts humming the theme to the Olympics, da . . . da . . . da da . . . da . . . da da, strips naked, takes a victory lap, and ceremoniously lights Fleet Hollinger on fire. Witnesses say that given the horror of it, it was actually a beautiful sight. Luckily, before the rest of the place went up, the Barnheisels were able to beat Fleet out and drag him through a window. He's going to be fine, except in all those ways that he won't be.

"The point is, we are a community, and we are going to bounce back from this stronger than ever and committed to whatever it is we are supposed to be committed to. Proof of that is the dedication with which the residents are fleeing town. So you see, a lot of good is coming out of this. It's the best thing that could happen, and I hope it never happens again."

DONNIE LARSON

"Look, I'm not sayin' I don't like money. I've never said it. I've never claimed it, and I hope I didn't give that impression. It certainly wasn't my intention. Now, I got to admit, when I heard that there may be some monetary form of money to be distributed amongst the population, I have to admit my interest peaked. I'm not ashamed of that. Money has gotten' me out of more than a few jams. If you offer it to me, I'm gonna take it. That doesn't make me a bad guy. It doesn't make me a hero. I am the last person to sing my praises, especially

when it comes to money. Sometimes money and me don't see eye to eye. I know what could happen if I get my hands on some money. I'm not gonna lie about it. What good would it do me? The truth is, I've done some things with money I'm not so proud of, but I'm not ashamed of it. I just wouldn't want anybody to know about it. I wouldn't want it printed in the paper. I wouldn't want it read at church. Let's just say that one time I got my hands on a large amount of money and a lot of people got hurt. And that is all I'm going to say about it. It's an old story; everybody knows about it, I just don't want to talk about it. The point is, I'd like some money.

"Now, when I heard we weren't getting any money, I have to admit, I was a little disappointed. Now, I don't have anything against towns. I love the idea of us being a town, but evidently there is a fair amount of effort to being a town, and I just don't know if I'm up to the job. I just know through experience I'm just the last person I would trust with any responsibility. That's just the way things are.

"Now, I don't know what happened, or who did what to cause Representative Farber to not tear down our dam. I certainly don't want to point any fingers. It doesn't matter whose fault it was. Nobody's in trouble, we just need to find out who is responsible and go after him, and I'll lead the charge. I would just like to apologize to Representative Farber if he was offended in some way. If you are reading this, sir, I just want you to know I'm sorry for anything I might have done or any way I might have contributed to your change of heart. I guess I'm speaking specifically about that word I painted on your car. I know it's an ugly word. I shouldn't have done it. It's just a word I grew up with and I don't mean it as a personal attack on you or your family. I thought we had the money in our pockets, and that made me happy, and when I'm happy I celebrate, you can ask anybody, that's not a secret. Anyway, I had a few drinks. I don't know how it happened, but the next thing I know is I painted that word on your car, it's nobody's fault, these things happen, nobody is to blame. I just want to say, sir, that I'm sorry, and would you please tear down our dam?"

JULIAN CHILDS

"I don't know why violence always rears its nasty head. After Representative Farber declared his intentions and shortly before Fleet Hollinger was set ablaze, I suggested that the group assume characters based on animals and work through their aggression and frustration through role-playing. Of course, they didn't want to assume the roles of animals, they'd rather play characters like 'the knife-wielding maniac' or 'the pipe-wielding maniac.'

"These people are completely undirectable. I know when my rabbits get out of control I stamp my feet and clap my hands until they come to attention. Or sometimes I'll eat one in full view of the others. It helps to drive home the point. But I don't think I can justify cannibalizing a townsperson. So I tried something else that occasionally works with my ensemble. The Shock Treatment. I simply do something shocking or silly or shockingly silly to get their attention. In this case I turned my back on them and spoke to a wall! It just came to me. I said, 'Hello, Wall. How are you today? I don't know why they're not listening either, Wall, but it's their loss, because I have a lot of interesting things to say. Say, Wall? What is that sharp pain in my ribs? And while you're mulling that one over, see if you can figure out why I'm on fire. Oh God, the pain, Wall. Make it stop!'

"As soon as my hair grows back, I'm pressing charges."

Those are accounts of some of the town members present at the town meeting. But, I'm sorry, I don't think I could sit on what I have to say, and I am not planning to any longer. Excuse me if this next passage is not up to par. I'm

still attempting to piece together the shattered shards of the last couple of days. Now you have read the accounts by townspeople of the celebratory melee. My editor felt I should include those eyewitness accounts instead of my own account saying, and I quote: "Even given that your writing is, at its best, a jumbled, incomprehensible mess, this next section stands out like a turd in a shit hole." Close quote. Well, Hyperion Books, thank you for your support. In retort, I would like to respond with this: The author cannot be constrained by the limitations of the English language. I'm sorry if my sentences don't fit into your neat little package of Subject, Verb, Object, but I've got a story to tell here, and sometimes stories don't fit into neat little packages. With that in mind, let me go back and describe the first of the last things I remember.

Darkness. Flickering light . . . darkness. Hot stink of fear. Throbbing, pounding, agony . . . Darkness . . .

There. That wasn't so painful, was it? Crucial to my story? Perhaps not. Thematically related to the rest of this book? No. Twelve words? Undeniably. Consider for the moment if I had relented and chosen not to include those words. Would the book make any less sense? I don't think so. Would the reader feel cheated to find out they were not included? I doubt it. Then why include them? Well, consider for the moment something other than the thing I asked you to consider for the moment a moment ago. If these words were not included it would be tantamount to me admitting that my editor knows more than me.

As for what happened after Farber's announcement and why, I still have no insight. I have to say I'm bewildered by the reaction of the town. Puzzled. So puzzled in fact that my confusion itself is dumbfounded. Let's go through this again: a town is on the brink of annihilation, it has one month to save itself, and when all looks lost, I come up with a lifesaving suggestion that indeed saves the town. Why are these people unhappy?! Am I missing something here?! It's almost as if they weren't ever really interested in becoming a town. The worst part is, they seem to be blaming me. All of a sudden I am being shunned. I'm an outcast. Nobody will talk to me. It's just like *The Scarlet Letter*, the only difference being that my isolation is due to narrow-minded people refusing to think as individuals condemning an innocent without having accurate information. In *The Scarlet Letter*, the woman is shunned because she is a harlot. She deserved what she got. I think she came on to a priest or something. I don't remember; I only saw the movie once. I checked it out from the library. That's right, a movie from the library! For my money, it was hard to be excited about libraries until they started checking out movies. I can't wait until the switchover is complete. What better way to show the obsoleteness of a book than by setting it next to a DVD? I'm glad libraries are leading the charge against books.

Getting back to Wigfield, I don't know how, after all that we have been through, they could just ignore me. How am I supposed to finish this book without other people's words? I'm tempted to slap a big fat The End on it and call it a day. But I can't allow myself to do it. I just don't feel like I have the complete story. I'm pretty sure the complete story is only a specific number of words away. I cannot imagine what I could have done to alienate these people. Perhaps now that they have what they want from me, I'm no longer useful to them. I'm like a plastic jug you might toss into a landfill after the liquid is gone, or a car battery you might leave at a playground after it no longer holds a charge, or perhaps they think of me as a spent plutonium rod left to be safely buried under a water supply. Who knows? But the odd thing is, as I mentioned before, these people don't seem to have what they want. Their faces seem sullen. Their expressions appear expressionless. I decided that the best plan of action was to force contact. I needed to get into the minds of these people. I could spend all the time I want thinking, but thinking does not get a book written. Besides, it's a lot of work.

I needed to see Fleet Hollinger, so I devised a clever plan. I went to his office. It seemed that if anybody could give me insight into what he was thinking, it would be him.

I met with Fleet in the back of his used auto parts shop. He looked reasonably well for a man whose head was recently set ablaze. He had scars covering his pate like moss. I would liken them to lichen. I sat across from him as he leaned back in his chair, hands folded behind his head, his feet resting on the top of his desk, cigarette dangling from his lips, his lean frame engaged in a fierce exchange of violent reprisals with his bloated midriff, his hands tightly clenched in loose fists rhythmically pounding his kneecaps, his feet planted firmly on the floor, his eyes glazed yet fiery hot like a coffee mug plucked freshly like a flower from a kiln, his hands cupped nonchalantly over his generous waist, his feet splayed about, looking every inch the used auto parts salesman, as befits a mayor. We sat in eerie silence for what seemed like a long time but was actually a long while. He glared at me as if I had somehow betrayed him. I broke through the silence, like an overeager skater might break through the ice on an October pond, my words grasping blindly for some response like that same skater clawing madly at the edges of the icy hole he fell through, until my words floated lifeless and alone in the frigid conversational waters.

I confessed to Fleet that I was confused about the mood of the town. I didn't understand why people were pulling away. What happened to the friendliness and neighborliness that I had worked so hard to exploit? What happened to the open amiability, that can-do spirit, my free meals? But Fleet just continued to stare. I gave him examples. People are refusing my requests for interviews and lodging. Last night, at what I consider to be a diner, the homeowner refused to serve me. The once affable strippers used to seem pleased when I tucked a little something inside their G-strings, now they insist that something be money. This isn't about me. I'm just worried about the town and what it's not doing for me.

Fleet remained silent. I was wondering if my words were getting through to him. It was as if I had landed on some primitive island like Puerto Rico or Mexico and was attempting to communicate with the local chieftain, whose only language was the musical birdlike hoots uttered by himself and his fellow head shrinkers who, clad only in animal loincloths, playing bone flutes stuck through the holes in their noses, were busy chasing their many wives around the cannibal cook pot. I became frustrated. My rage turned into fury. I began to hurl a stream of unedited words hoping to overwhelm his reticence with sheer quantity. I told him I believed the town was acting like a village of spoiled children.

"I don't understand!" I screamed. "I've seen towns react better after their homes were destroyed by hurricanes, or buried by earthquakes, and all they got was federal disaster relief payments to soothe their loss!" Finally, Fleet cocked an eyebrow. Perhaps my diatribe was wearing him down. I hoped so, because it was certainly wearing me down. I continued.

"But you people confound me! You still have your town!"

"If it where up to I," me said, "I would be out celebrating this glorious victory! Why, I'd march straight up to the dam and throw the biggest party this town has ever seen! I would have music! I would have a buffet! I would cap the day off with a large display of fireworks right at the base of the dam!"

Yes, something I was saying was definitely having some sort of effect. I noticed some glimmer of response. I felt my words softening the target like a missile strike on a reluctant village. I continued with my assault, fueled by the knowledge that I was making headway. I reiterated, "A celebration to end all celebrations! Music, food, topped off with a magnificent fireworks display right at the base of the dam! Let the whole world know about our victory!"

I stared into Fleet's eye, breathing heavy with the excited anticipation of afterthought. He arched the other eyebrow and slowly sat up in his chair. He leaned into the desk and took a breath. He then spoke his first words.

"So, tell me more about this fireworks display."

"Well," I said, "think 'A Hiroshima of Joy'! We could detonate the whole area in a demonstration of our victory! Think of the finale we could have! After the initial choreographed fireworks display, maybe set to music, we could gather all the leftovers, sort of pile it up at the bottom of the dam, and wind one huge fuse around them and let 'er rip"!

He spoke again, "I like your celebration idea. Take me through it again, slowly. Especially the finale."

CHAPTER TWENTY-FOUR

AND that's how I became the chairman of the Wigfield Victory Celebration Committee. Fleet, Hoyt, and Burchal buried their differences, and then buried Burchal, who never really recovered from Lenare's accidental multiple stab wounds. Fleet and Hoyt would be the fireworks committee and acquire what promised to be the largest collection of explosives ever assembled in the state since the construction of the Bulkwaller Dam.

I decided to go out into the town to gauge the excitement about the impending celebration.

JULIAN CHILDS

"I love a party. When I hear tell of one, step back and watch the tootsies, 'cause I'm coming through. I love planning them. When my little sniffer caught wind that Wigfield was throwing a celebration, you could have knocked me over with a peacock's tail. I immediately stamped my little piggies (and you know the sound clogs can make) and insisted that I co-chair the party committee. It is a travesty that I even needed to beg, to humiliate and degrade myself, to stoop to such horrible depths to be part of a party planning committee when it's so obvious, I mean fourteen-point-leaded-crystal clear, that I am the Mother Goose of party planning! I know how to prepare for a party, I know who to invite, and more important, I know who not to invite. Trust me, it's all about the mix. I know how to decorate; I know how to kick it off. And I know how to keep the party going. Never turn the music down, never turn the lights up, and most important, no fatties! A party is very similar to theater. Both involve a lot of preplanning, assigned seating, rehearsing, getting your lines down, costumes, and anonymous sex. I'm already making lists in my head of things we'll need.

Two-sided tape

Large wooden spools

Folding chairs

Mylar balloons! (Buy string)

Call caricaturist (Dillard?)

Replace bulb in tanning booth

Think of things

Tiki torches

Mosquito netting

Bathing suit

Charcoal

Chips, chips, chips!

Japanese lanterns

Hot sauce

Floating candles

Something to float candles in

Hose

Popsicle sticks

Hot-glue gun

Mechanical bull

Whippets/rush/poppers? (Call Cooter)

Personalized beer cozies (Wigfield Wigout?)

Mirrored ball

T. P.

Ice

Citronella

Leaf blower

Remember to comb out brush

Get some rest!

"This has got to be the party to end all parties! I have a feeling the people of this town, even Lenare, will take a little more notice of what I have to offer. I'm planning to drape the dam à la the artist Christo, in giant cloth sheets, and then cinch it with rope like a girdle. It will be my statement! Because, if there is one thing that's sticking around this town, it's two things: the dam, and me!"

HOYT GEIN

"I'm excited, hell yeah. Fleet made me the field marshal of the fireworks display. Evidently they think I'm the right man for the job, which they should because, make no mistake about it, I'm the master of flame. The only thing I respect as much as things that burn are things that explode. Viewing from a distance is highly recommended. Might want to wear a raincoat. Let's just say you might want to watch from high ground. Let's just also say most of the show will take place around the load-bearing sections of the dam. Sometimes implosion is as beautiful as explosion, don't you think? The point is, I'd get your celebratin' done quick, and then hightail it to the end of town, because believe you me, once I kick off the show, it's gonna be nothing but asses and elbows down here."

MAE ELLA PADGETT

"Yeah, yeah, yeah. Celebration. I don't understand. I'll play along, but what a waste of time, money, and funds. I mean, come on, who are we fooling? We're all adults. It's all a bunch of baloney. I say let's cut the cold cuts and go straight to the fireworks barrage. I mean, there is not a person in this town who isn't packed and ready to go, except for maybe that fag with the rabbits, and Mayor McFudge. I don't know why we have to go mingle, standing in the path of that fireworks display. I know I said I'd do my part, and I will. I know the celebratory blitzkrieg isn't supposed to start until dusk, but once you put a fuse in Hoyt Gein's hands there's no telling what's gonna happen. He's like a fox in a refrigerator full of chicken meats. I just don't get it. But so be it. I'll show up. I'll drink from the punch bowl. I'll pose for a picture, but you can be damn well sure I'm going to have my escape route planned."

DONNIE LARSON

"I done my share of celebrating, I'm not ashamed. And yes, from time to time I've crossed the line, and what started out as a celebration turned into something that can best be described as a violent free-for-all with party favors. But the bottom line is I like to party. I'm a party kind of guy, ask anybody, they'll all say the same thing. They will say Donnie loves to party. And I do! I love to party, that's not a crime, although I have done some time as a result, but that's not a crime either. You can bet I'll be there. I'll be right in the center of things. Fleet has me helping with the fireworks show. I'm supposed to pack fireworks into some holes that Hoyt is going to drill into the dam, or something. I'm a doer not a don'ter. But after that it's all about the party, and I'm going to party to the full letter of the law."

LENARE

"Let's just say I got my concerns. I'm on crowd control. Now, your crowd is very similar to your herd of antelope. If you're lucky, you get them moving all together in a pack. But if somethin' startles 'em, you know, something loud and bright like, let's say, a fireworks show, you got problems. Fight-or-flight kicks in, and then I've got no choice but to cut the leader from the herd and try to corral the rest into the right direction. God, animals are stupid. They will do anything I force them to. That's why I put up pine breaks with sharp edges all the way up to the high ground. It slows 'em down. I filled the path with lots of turns. I learned that from the slaughterhouse. If you have enough turns, then one cow can't see the tail end of the other so he has no idea what's comin'. And let me tell you, they don't know what's comin'. Once I get the herd to the higher ground it's my job to keep them there, and keep them calm, while the, uh, finale rushes by."

CHAPTER TWENTY-FIVE

WIGFIELD WIGOUT

Hello, Mr. and Mrs. America, this is Russell Hokes coming to you live via my tape recorder reporting from this the first annual Wigfield Town Charter Celebration, otherwise known as the Wigfield Wigout. It's just about dusk, and I suspect people will begin gearing up for the fireworks display. There's been a great turnout. What a splendid day! What a day to remember! With the exception of four or five horrible things, of which I choose not to speak for risk of sullying a sullyless report, the celebration is coming off without any major hitch, but I will say Donnie Larson's blatant disregard for the law should be illegal. The party grounds look wonderfully festive, thanks to my team of Julian Childs. Due to what he described as budgetary concerns, Julian Childs overslept and was forced to simplify his admirably ambitious party plans. In lieu of streamers, balloons, and a salsa band, piles of burning used tires and strippers are scattered around the grounds in order to achieve his new stripper-and-used-tire theme.

Everybody from town made an appearance. Fleet Hollinger showed up early, scurrying through the crowd shaking hands and sharing knowing winks with other celebrants. He is amazingly resilient, having rebounded from a close race for mayors that ended in flames, and a parade protest against the state that ended in flames, the tragic loss of his sheriff (also to flames), and a flaming scalp. This is a man whose will to survive is probably only outweighed by his struggle to live. Other town luminaries include Dottie Fore and Mae Ella Padgett, who seem to have buried their differences by agreeing to hate each other. Mae Ella looks beautiful in an outfit she fashioned just for the occasion. She's right here. Mae Ella, why don't you describe your party dress for us.

"Well, let's just say fashion wasn't my biggest concern, but I'll tell you this much, the material is both flame retardant and buoyant. You know, just in case."

Thank you, Ms. Padgett. And I see Dottie Fore is resplendent in a fireman's jacket and life preserver.

Hoyt Gein brought Mayor Charles Halstead, who is being allowed to roam free for the occasion, heading straight for the sweets table.

Dillard Rankin is here with Carla Hollinger. From the looks of their gentle groping and tentative probing, I'd say that they are now clearly an item.

Giant lettering has been hung from the dam itself, spelling out the words WIGFIELD WIGOUT.

The excitement builds. Hoyt Gein is moving toward the base of the dam carrying fuses, a torch, and other explosive delights. I can only imagine what flaming wonders will emerge from the deep shafts bored directly into the face of the dam. The bulk of the crowd now seems to be retreating with anticipation. Like native anglers protecting the whereabouts of the prime fishin' hole, they must be privy to some ideal viewing location unbeknownst to me, although it would be hard to imagine a better perch than where I'm standing, smack dab in the middle of this former river bottom. Why, just the sight of this mammoth concrete abutment is enough to stir the soul of the most jaded cosmopolite. Think of it! Were it not for the vigilance of the Bulkwaller Dam, the waters it holds in check would descend on me like the Angel of Death, crushing and rending all in its path without thought or mercy. This very spot on which I stand would be a Watery Grave.

From the impressive clip the townspeople are moving at, it is clear that they are as eager for the colorful sky spectacle to begin as I am. Just the thought of fireworks brings back a flood of memories from my days as a youngster! I'll never forget those steamy July nights, lightning bugs buzzing about, driving back from Kentucky and crossing the state line with a load of explosives in the trunk of my Firebird. Oh, how the little children used to swarm around my bumper like refugees around a food drop, clutching three months' allowance in their tiny fists. How they would scramble for my gaily colored roman candles, or squeal in delight for a box of Black Cat Aerial Rampage mortar shells. Their little eyes would light up at the sight of the High-Torque Comet barrage, or the Pro Mag Dedigitizer, and of course you had to show up pretty early to get your hands on my number one seller, the Flashpoint Microfuse Eye-Level Mayhem barrage (with Atomic Fallout). I operated a pretty lucrative little business until I was shut down by the authorities, who seemed more interested in protecting their mailboxes and cats than letting small children celebrate America the way George Washington intended them to. If there is one thing I've learned in life, it's once somebody's kid loses a few fingers, that person should not be seated on your jury.

I'm impressed! Hoyt Gein seems to be really taking his time and care setting up the show. I, for one, appreciate the art in organizing a successful display. The mixture of colors and styles, varying the rockets so they explode low and high, all coming together in a ballet of fiery Armageddon, takes a certain skill. Of course, the real trick is to culminate in an ear-shattering finale. The whole thing gives me goose bumps! And what more glorious night for a fire-works display could we have? The cloud from the mercury runoff pit has floated south, and the thick gray mist from the lead dispersal plant has mostly dissipated, leaving a clear view of the dam. Wait a minute; I seem to have lost sight of Hoyt Gein. Perhaps he has gone for more supplies. Oh, I hope he doesn't make us wait too long. The anticipation of what I am expecting to happen is unbearable. Okay, something is happening. I just caught a whiff of sulfur in the air. Always a good sign that something is about to blow. Ah! There's Hoyt! Up in that tree. What's he doing up there?

It's exploding! It's exploding! The whole dam is exploding! I have been knocked to the ground by the terrible explosion. It's fire and it's crashing! The dam is crashing! Get away! Get away! It's falling and it's fire! Oh, the humanity! I can't talk! I can't breathe! The dam is a mass of smoking rubble. What's this? What fury hath hell unleashed now? Water is crashing through the smoking wreckage! Water water water! I don't know if I can go on! Honest, I can hardly breathe. Oh Lord! Julian Childs has just been swept away in the watery barrage, hastily attempting to lash his bevy of screaming rabbits into a makeshift life raft! I'm moving with the current now . . . rushing past town buildings . . . Tit Time . . . Sawyer's Wreckage Emporium . . . The Bacon Strip . . . the water batters these establishments, dismantling them as if they were just ramshackle structures fashioned from plywood and tin. I don't know what to say, this is the worst fireworks accident I've ever wit-nessed. The entire town is being submerged. Oh, the poor people! Who lived? Who died? Who, like me, was caught unawares in the fury of this watery hell? I see them now on the ridge top. Who lived? They all did. Oh, God love them for their brave hearts as they laugh and clap and hug each other in a vain attempt to stay strong in the face of their numbing grief. They seem to have escaped with nothing more than everything they own. Suitcases hastily stacked at their feet, I assume to be used as sand bags should the cruel torrent defy physics and reach that high. I'm sorry, I cannot go on . . . the town is in ruins . . . no longer will the words come . . . no strength to swim . . . must keep tape deck above water level . . . also must keep head above water level . . . so many things to keep dry . . . going down . . . going down . . .

CHAPTER TWENTY-SIX
Aftermath

IF it weren't for the courageous buoyancy of what was soon to become Mayor Charles Halstead's corpse, I wouldn't be here and this book would never be finished. Unless of course what my editor has read up to now seems complete to her, in which case I beg her to put the manuscript down NOW and CALL me! I would gladly stop working, because what comes next is pretty difficult to write and, I would imagine, just as difficult to read.

All right, brace yourselves, here we go.

Wigfield Is No More.

In place of that majestic strand of concrete, asphalt, and cinder block is the chilling sight of Nature Unchecked! Like a primitive Neanderthal ape-man of olden times, peeking furtively around the protective cover of a dinosaur carcass at a wild incomprehensible new world, so do we modern hu-mans stand, aghast and agog on the banks of this vengeful torrent, not quite sure what to make of this strange new watery land that was once our home. Oh, how the skyline has changed, or rather disappeared. What a hideous, almost obscene transformation of the landscape. Where once stood Burchal Sawyer's modern marvel of twisted steel and reclaimed auto carcasses, there is now only rippling water whose banks are fowled by fowl. Where once young ladies soothed the souls of weary truckers with candid glimpses of their proud and mighty tenderloin, there is now but a spawning ground for the amoral trout. There is almost no evidence that man was ever here.

But amid all the watery destruction, one thing that could never be submerged is the Wigfield spirit! Not so fast, Water! This kind of small-town spirit has a floatability factor of *Titanic* proportions! It has been said, most recently by me, that time heals all wounds. Well, these people have made short work of it. In the time that it takes most people to change into their grieving black, the people of Wigfield have bounced back as if their souls were made out of Superballs. Maybe the most important factor in their speedy recovery is their great good fortune. The mind reels at the fact that given a disaster of this proportion, almost every member of the town survived, and not only that, they were able to miraculously salvage nearly every possession! God has smiled on these people, at least from one side of his mouth, because from the other side he was clearly spitting. Amid all this mournful merriment, one agonizing question remains: What now? That question may never be answered.

CHAPTER TWENTY-SEVEN

I needed an answer. I decided to find Fleet Hollinger. As fate would have it, Fleet happened to be looking for me. I was briskly escorted by two of Fleet's neckless protégés to Fleet's makeshift compound. Fleet was loading everything he owned into a caravan of new trucks he had recently purchased.

"What now, Fleet," I said. "What happens now?"

"Funny you should ask. Well, here's the deal. I've talked to the boys down at the Federal Emergency Management Agency, and apparently we qualify for disaster relief, thank the Lord, and believe you me, this has come as quite a surprise to all of us. Here's the rub. The only thing that stands in the way of the forsaken people of the town of Wigfield from receiving just compensation for what was clearly . . . a . . . uh . . ."

"An act of God?" I interjected.

"Act of God! Yes. You took the words right out of my gobber. I don't know what God was thinking. Anyway, as I was saying, the only thing we need, in order to get what is justifiably coming to us, is this little written account of the tragedy by an impartial third-party witness who is not a town resident and will in no way benefit financially from money or monies distributed from the aforementioned federal agency. But jeez, where are we going to find one of those? Too bad, we were so close!"

I saw his quandary as he placed one of his meaty yet companionable arms around my shoulders and gave me a brotherly embrace. Where, I thought to myself? Where indeed? Then it struck me. Third-party account? Why, I could be that account. The third-party person could be me! I turned to Fleet, "I could be your impartial third-party account!"

"Hold the phone! Wait a second. Could it be? Noooo."

"Yes! It could be me!"

"You know something, it could be! I never thought of that, but, yes, it could be!"

"But what exactly would I write?"

"Hell, I don't know. I suppose it could be something like, 'I witnessed the spontaneous implosion of a federal dam due to some previously unknown preexisting structural flaw that through no known triggering mechanism of the town of Wigfield resulted in a catastrophic failure of the Bulkwaller Memorial Dam, causing the complete and utter destruction of property, livestock, livelihood, any and all claimable assets, and future wage-earning potential, plus grief and suffering.' Period. I'd say something exactly like that, double-spaced on acid-free paper and delivered to me by, say, an hour should suffice. I don't know, am I being too vague? I mean, do what you want. Hey, wait a minute, maybe you could just sign this letter right here!"

His thick-browed associate handed him a piece of paper with writing on it.

"Hell, it pretty much says the same thing."

Well, I signed that typewritten paper and handed it back to Fleet. It was really such a small gesture considering how much the people of this town had suffered.

Later that afternoon I positioned myself near the entrance to the highway to watch the procession of displaced Wigfieldeans move toward a new life. Until this moment, I hadn't realized how much like family they seemed. As I watched these people, these persons, my family, move toward tomorrow, today, away from all our yesterdays, I could not help but feel like a proud papa whose children have outgrown the nest because it was flooded.

It is often said, but rarely heard, that it is easier to leave a loved one without saying good-bye, which clearly explains why none of my surrogate relatives spoke a single parting word to me. I understand. Enough said. Their silence spoke volumes, almost as if they had showered me with tears, words of farewell, and parting gifts. These people must have been in the depths of separation anxiety, seeing that they were unable to attempt even an acknowledging head nod in response to the many cheerful waves I offered. As they sped off, fighting the urge to note my presence, I didn't envy their next few months. God, how they must be going to miss me. If only there were dozens and dozens of me, or at least a home-game version of me that I could hand out as consolation prizes that they could take to their new homes and play so they could feel I was with them always. But, alas, all that remain are memories of what once was, that, like wounds, can only be healed by the antibacterial action of time.

As I write these words through my own personal flood of tears, I wonder what will become of these people. I also wonder why their story ended before my book did. How is it that they have all moved on, yet I'm still writing? If there were any justice in the world, they wouldn't have packed up until right around word 50,000. The truth is, I don't even know where I'm at anymore, word-count-wise. Somehow, somewhere around 40,000, I let myself become distracted. I became too personally involved with my subject matter, which is always the most mistake a journalist can make. So now, instead of mailing off my neatly packed, completed manuscript to my impatient editor, I'm simply dropping words into a numberless void without any concrete goal.

How can I ever hope to finish this job? How, indeed, had I ever finished any job? Threats were always helpful, but in this case they were plentiful— but they still weren't bringing any closure to this verbal treadmill. Maybe my previous occupational experience held some hints. What Universal Truths could I glean from those carefree days painting center lines for the highway department?

1. Paint a straight line

OK. I can do that. What is the "line" here? Two points make a line. What's the point of this book? Nothing there. Next?

2. Go slow

No problem. You can't go much slower than this. But even a crawl will eventually take you off the end of the gangplank. I've got no subjects left to interview, nothing left to observe. Just me and my talent.

So . . . so cold.

3. Keep plenty of paint on your brush

What the hell does that mean? What am I going to do? Think! Think? That's the problem right there. I'm overthinking this whole thing. Back on the highway we kept things simple. Just show up in the morning, grab a brush pole, and hang off the back of a truck in a harness slapping paint on hot asphalt for eight hours. You couldn't overthink that job. You could barely think at all. Your mind would be wiped clean by the hypnotizing blur of the passing pavement, the hissing black noise of tires on tar whose fumes would infuse your very bones and smoke your brain until it was hard and dark like a country ham. It was the opposite of experience. Awareness itself was eaten by these black mindless wormhole days through which you passed, a numb automaton, to Friday after Friday and the flickering moment of consciousness when the paycheck was pressed into your outstretched hand.

God, I miss that job! If I ever scrape this book off my boot, I'm going to beg my foreman to take me back.

But crawling on my belly isn't going to feed the insatiable maw of my editor. I suppose I could always try to answer the question that I posed in this book way back when my publisher posed it. The question, of course, was, "Why are America's small towns fading like autumn leaves on the branches of America's proud pine tree?" Fair enough. I just wrote a whole book about a small town. I must have an answer. At this point any answer would do. I mean, why on earth would somebody write a book if it couldn't at least resolve the one simple query it posed? Because when it boils down to it, this book isn't just about filling up pages with words, or fulfilling contracts, it is about looking into the heart of one town balanced on the edge of destiny's knife. It is about shining a light on the dark midnight of America's soul. And if by doing that I can help explain one of our nation's greatest tragedies and apply that understanding to other small towns caught in History's crosshairs, maybe all of this will have been worth it. So, Devil take the derriere, here goes: The reason America's small towns are disappearing is this: For many . . . 50,000! I've hit 50,000! If you'll forgive me for a moment, I just need to catch my breath. Okay, I'm gathering myself. I decided to go back and do a word count, and I've passed 50,000! Take that, Hyperion! I bet you thought I'd never finish!

Now pay up!

REDEDICATION

IN retrospect, this book wouldn't have been possible without the generous contribution, kind support, and bemused detachment of too many people to name. Namely:

The tenacious, simple, heart-hearted residents of Wigfield, whose support went beyond the point of assistance and encouragement. Their involvement, given that much of the book is in their own words, could almost be called a collaboration. I would like to stress *almost* a collaboration, and not an *actual* collaboration. Hopefully this will clear up any future debates about book royalties.

RE-REDEDICATION

I would like to dedicate this book to all the good people in charge of nominating books for the Pulitzer Prize. Now, I don't know exactly who you people are, but I do know that whoever hands out those Pulitzer Prizes is on the stick. They are a sharp crowd who I would wager are also very attractive. So once again, kudos to the whole Pulitzer crew. They do a great job, and by saying this I mean to take none of the glory away from the wonderful men and women working at the National Book Award. Thank you.

Amy, Paul, and Stephen would very much like to thank the following people:

EVELYN McGEE, for being more organized than the three of us put together. VICTORIA FARRELL and ANTONIA XEREAS, for the costume design and styling including the rabbit's costumes.

TONY LONGORIA, HISHAM BHAROOCHA, LAUREN SMITH, JOSH GEURTSEN, CONN BRATTAIN, and KELLI HARTLINE, who without their generosity and support this book would be picture-less.

STEVEN PERFIDIA KIRKAHM, JIM CRAWFORD, DAN SHARP and DAVID H. LAWRENCE, for their ability to manipulate hair. SCOTT McMAHAN and WHAT'S HIS NAME, for makeup and disguises.

PETERNELLE VAN ARSDALE, editor and schoolmarm. NATALIE KAIRE, who we talk to every day. TRACY FISHER, for talking to us every day, and always, CAGNEY and ANN.